The Migdal Eder Mystery

A novel based
on the Christmas story

Peter Smith

LIGHTHOUSE
PUBLISHING

Published by Lighthouse Publishing Limited

ISBN: 978-1910848340

A catalogue record for this book is available from the British Library.

Bible quotes are taken from The Message. Copyright © 1993, 1994,
1995, 1996, 2000, 2001, 2002. Used by permission of NavPress
Publishing Group.

Cover design by Esther Kotecha, EKDesign

Typeset by Angela Selfe

Printed and bound in the UK

My thanks to

God – for the prompt to write

Matthew and Luke – for foundation information

Dr. Chuck Missler – his incredible research.

Jackie Smith, Lynda Elwell and Phil Gardner for
proof reading and David Powell (my publisher)
for his support and advice throughout this project.

introduction

Like most parents, I have been entertained many times at Christmas by the traditional Christmas story as performed by eight-year-old children. Always good fun, with the not-so-wise men tripping over each other whilst a lamb sits and cries because he wanted to be a king! Although fun to watch, these dramas never bear much resemblance to the original story. So what really may have happened?

As a young teenager, I can remember looking at the moon while cycling quickly along the road by my home, and then stopping to look at the moon again. As I expected, it had not changed position. I thought about this for some time, and knowing that stars are considerably further away from the earth than the moon, I had a question: How could a star come to rest over the house where Jesus was? I had always accepted that the accounts in Matthew and Luke were divinely inspired, and therefore were definitely correct although they had several differences.

Then at the 'Spring Harvest' teaching and worship event one year, I heard the testimony of the New Zealand star! As a result of this testimony, I wrote a Christmas play for adults to perform, and for children to watch. This play was performed in Ely, UK.

Subsequently, I heard the Christmas presentation by Dr. Chuck Missler, and this short novel has been the result.

In this novel, I have woven the two Bible accounts together into a flowing account of what may have happened around the first Christmas. I have also tried to filter out those aspects of Christmas that are based on folklore rather than the Bible, and I have incorporated more of the Jewish tradition.

There cannot be many people who believe that Jesus was born on 25th December, but when was He born? Obviously we cannot be certain when it was, but from the dates commonly suggested, I have selected the one that I think is the most likely date. Ironically, that date is based on the Bible itself, and on the importance God attaches to His feast days. Traditional Jews believe that the Messiah will reveal Himself at the start of the year on the Feast of Trumpets, or Rosh Hashanah. The Feast of Trumpets is the most holy feast in the Jewish calendar, and it always takes place in late September or early October; the perfect time for the birth of Jesus.

Jesus was baptised to enter the Melchizedek priesthood (Matthew 3:13-15) which would have happened at the exact age of thirty. His ministry is generally held to have been 3½ years. We also know that he

6

was crucified at Passover. This seals his birth at Rosh Hashanah.

As for the stable? I have always thought of Jesus being born in a sheepfold under, or inside a Bethlehem house. However, my research revealed another possibility, which is the one I elected to use in my story. Which is the correct birthplace scenario? We will never know, but I have tried to create a mini novel based totally on the Bible and also on the results of my research.

Although it is usual for characters to be described in a narrative, I have deliberately not attempted to describe either Joseph or Mary. People often have pictures in their minds as to what these characters look like, and I did not want to spoil the image a person may have of these two characters. Surely Mary (or Mariam) always wears a blue top over a white undergarment, doesn't she?!

My main source of information has been the Bible. Most of my other research has come from various internet sites, especially the YouTube presentation 'The Christmas Story' based on the research of Dr. Chuck Missler. If you wish to deepen your own understanding of Christmas, I strongly recommend watching Dr Missler's Christmas story, published by the Koinonia Institute

chapter one

Joseph examined the table which was almost finished. He turned it around, and carefully studied his craftsmanship. He was satisfied. It was for someone special, so he wanted it to be really good. He looked around his tidy workshop, noting that everything was in its place. His father, Jacob, had been a good teacher!

"An untidy work shop shows you have an untidy mind," Jacob had insisted. "If you want to follow in my footsteps as one of the best carpenters in Nazareth, you must maintain high standards!"

Joseph had done his best to be obedient to his father. Jacob had a very good reputation in the district, and Joseph was determined to follow in his footsteps. After all, if he failed, he would have to rely on the other tasks a tekton or carpenter had to do. That would mean cutting the long timbers for roof beams, and cutting stones to make the walls of houses. Cutting timbers and stones was good work through which he could earn a living, but Joseph was far more interested in the craftsmanship of a skilled carpenter. There was something really satisfying about looking at a table or chair that he had made, especially when he saw it later being used and cared for by its new owner.

Jacob had been a good teacher, instructing him how to cut some of the stones they had needed to extend their workshop so that there would be space for both of them to work there. He had also cut some of the roof timbers required but, as he was quite young at the time, Jacob had done most of the heavy work. He was very pleased with his son and protégé, and Joseph had worked hard to develop his skills. Jacob had to admit that, if anything, Joe was now a better craftsman that he was! This pleased him as he would never have to worry about Joseph's future.

He was so pleased that his own father, Matthan, had encouraged him to develop the skill of carpentry. It was extremely hard work, especially when whole trees needed to be cut down. Being a nomadic people by nature, very few Israelites had settled down long enough to develop the skills and physical strength required of a carpenter. The most common skills the nomadic people had were tent-making, animal husbandry and making clothes.

Joseph had hand made the small collection of axe-like adzes that hung on nails around the workshop, each slightly different from the others. He had developed a real interest in making himself the best tools he could. He also had a collection of different iron and bronze saws. It took a lot of work to keep the saws sharp, as they blunted easily. He had these displayed on wooden frames fixed around the stone walls of the workshop.

He picked up his adze, and chipped gently at one of the table legs that was not quite as good as he wanted, then looked out through the doorway. The hot summer was now over, so working was a lot easier than it had been during the previous few months. The winter solstice was just months away, then there would be a few weeks with very cold evenings, some very cold days, and possibly even a little snow. There was often snow on the higher mountains, and it did very occasionally snow in Nazareth. Joseph was always pleased when winter had passed and the longer, warmer days of summer approached.

"Hello Joe," Mary called out from the doorway as she stepped into the workshop, "your mother asked me to drop some fresh fruit in to you for a snack."

"Thanks, my love." Joseph answered as he put the adze down.

Mary had been drawn to his workshop ever since she was a young girl. There was something nice about the smell of wood being cut, and she was also drawn to Joseph's kind nature. Initially she had looked in to watch him work, but as she grew older, she started to find herself being attracted to the man himself. Then, one afternoon, Joseph's mother had asked her if she was going to the workshop, and if she was, could she possibly take something for Joseph to save her the walk. Her heart had leapt with joy at having a real reason to visit the workshop and chat to Joseph. From then on, she would deliberately go past Jacob's house to see if there was anything she could take.

Joseph had always enjoyed Mary's visits. He liked this young girl who always called him Joe, and initially it gave him a reason to pause in his work and chat to a pretty young village girl. But as the years had passed, Mary had grown into a very attractive young woman. As a young teenager she had completed her bat mitzvah celebration, and so was now recognised as an adult. Then, a short time later, Joseph had taken her hands in his, to ask her if she would be his wife.

"Mary," he had said very sheepishly, "there's something I'd like to ask you." Mary had looked up coyly, hoping that Joseph might be about to make a personal request.

"I know I am a good few years older than you are, so I won't be upset if you don't want to give me permission."

"Permission for what?" Mary had answered, as she gave Joe an almost coquettish sideways look.

"Well . . ." Joseph hesitated. Did he really dare to ask Mary the next question? "Well . . ." he said again as he paused, "I would like to ask your father for permission to marry you."

"I wondered when you'd get around to asking me that!" Mary answered.

"You mean you'd be happy to marry me?" The excitement and surprise showed clearly in Joseph's expression.

"Of course I would! Can we go and ask him now?" Mary laughed eagerly as she grabbed his hand.

"I'm supposed to go and ask him myself," Joseph countered, "but I didn't want to ask him if you didn't want to marry me." Joe pulled back slightly as he spoke.

Mary smiled, "You didn't want to try to arrange things behind my back in case I didn't want to marry you. How thoughtful of you." She moved forward and gave Joseph a quick hug.

"And also, I didn't want to have to face up to your father if he had someone else in mind for you!" He gently pushed Mary away as he spoke. "I don't have permission yet," he added quietly

"You don't have to worry on that score," Mary answered. "Mother has known for ages how much you've meant to me, and I know she talks things over with father. If he'd had any objections, mother would have told me a long, long time ago." Mary was now totally confident of the outcome of the situation.

"That's a relief!" Joe answered as he allowed Mary to give him another hug. "But has he spoken to my parents yet? I mean, traditionally we aren't supposed to know anything, are we? Our parents are supposed to arrange everything!"

"I think he has," Mary continued. "My parents know my views on everything, and they know that a love marriage can be better than an arranged one." Her hug tightened around Joseph's waist.

"Yes, but love marriages are still very unusual." Joseph answered. He wanted to do everything correctly, although he didn't push Mary away this time.

"But you would be seen to be a good catch because you're not just an ordinary tekton, you're a skilled carpenter!" Mary answered confidently, "My children will be safe having you as their father. Actually I wouldn't mind betting that our parents have already got together about us! So shall we go now?"

Even with Mary's encouragement, Joseph was quite anxious at the prospect of having to ask Joachim and Anne for permission to marry Mary. But Mary was right! Her parents had a soft spot for Joseph, and her father agreed very easily to them getting married.

"So now" Mary exclaimed, "We'll have to arrange for our parents to meet and organise our formal engagement. Then we can all gather together and start planning for the wedding. Just before, or just after next summer should be about right, shouldn't it?"

The news of the engagement spread quite quickly through the rural community, and people started to look forward to the anticipated wedding that they expected to occur during the following summer.

However, Mary's dreams were shattered at just about the time of the winter solstice. After preparing some bread ready for baking so that there would be fresh bread for tea, she decided to sit down and continue sewing the clothes she was preparing ready for the marriage ceremony.

"I've got a little time while the bread cooks," she said to herself. "I don't want to waste it! Too much to do!" Suddenly she had the feeling that there was someone else in the room. She sat still for a moment, just listening – but the feeling did not go away. She turned her head and standing just behind her was a glowing figure.

The sewing fell from her lap as she gasped and sprung to her feet. "Who are you, and what do you want!" she exclaimed.

"Don't be afraid!" the figure said in a very gentle deep, rich voice. He was very tall, taller than anyone she knew with golden hair and striking blue eyes. He looked like any normal human man, except for the faint glow that surrounded him, and the love that seemed to flow out of him. His clothing was what she would expect to see the servant of a very high official wearing: a pure white robe that had neither crease nor blemish and a light shawl was draped over his shoulders.

"I ... I'm not afraid!" she stammered. "I know I should be terrified ... But I'm not! Who are you, sir?"

"I am Gabriel, and I bring you greetings from El Elyon!"

Mary stood frozen to the spot. Had she heard correctly? Had this strange visitor really come from the God of Abraham, Isaac and Jacob? How was it that God, YHWH, had sent a special messenger to her? After all, nothing had been recorded in the Torah for about four hundred years, so why should that change now?

"M ... me!" she finally stammered. "Who am I that YHWH should even know that I exist?"

The visitor held out his arms towards the baffled young lady, and Mary felt waves of love flowing from them all over her.

"Please don't be afraid of the news I have to give you." Gabriel said, speaking quite slowly so that Mary would hear clearly what he had to say.

"But sir . . ." Mary stammered. Trying to think was almost impossible while this powerful stranger was in the same room. Speaking was even more difficult!

"God is going to give you a child," the visitor continued. Mary relaxed a little more with this knowledge. Mary knew a number of wives who had never managed to produce a baby, and that was considered a bad sign, even a disgrace by some people! It was as if God had rejected them. Even her relative, Elizabeth, had never had a baby and she was now well past child-bearing age. It was with relief that Mary accepted this news.

"I hoped He would," Mary continued with obvious relief. "But I'm not getting married to Joseph for a few months yet." She paused whilst she considered the situation, then continued slowly, "Why is God telling me that He's going to bless our marriage before we are even married?"

"This is not going to be Joseph's baby," Gabriel continued. "He is going to be God's very own son!"

Mary thought carefully about Gabriel's message, then hesitantly asked, "I . . . I'm going to have God's baby . . .? But how?" She paused as she considered this seemingly impossible situation. "How can this be?" She sunk into a chair as she reflected on this amazing information. God – giving her a baby? She knew all life, and so all babies, came from God, but . . .

Gabriel cut into her thoughts. "You will have a baby boy, and you are to give Him the name 'Jesus'" Gabriel continued. "He will be great, and will be called the Son of the Most High. The Lord God will give Him the throne of David, and His kingdom will never end."

Mary began to think of having a baby with her husband Joseph – after they got married, of course. Joseph's baby would obviously be a special baby, possibly like Isaiah or one of the other prophets.

Then Gabriel cut in on her silent plans, "God will send His Holy Spirit to you, and you will find yourself pregnant. God can do all things. In fact, although your relative Elizabeth is past child-bearing age, she is also having a baby boy, and this is now the sixth month for her who was called barren! For with God nothing is impossible!"

Mary sat silently for a few moments considering everything she had heard. Could she really believe that this strange messenger was the angel, Gabriel? Could she really believe that God, somehow, was going to make her pregnant? Could she believe that this was not just a strange dream? She looked at Gabriel again. If he was who he said he was, and if these things were going to come true, who was she to argue with God?

"I am the Lord's servant," she finally said. "Let everything happen as He has said."

She put her hand on her stomach and looked down at it. Was she really going to have God's Son in her stomach? She looked up again, and found herself looking at an empty room. Had all this really happened? Had it been a dream? Then she thought about how she felt. She definiteiy felt different. She felt a lightness that was not natural. Something really had happened! She started to sing, quietly at first, but then with more volume as her happiness grew. She picked up her sewing again and continued from where she had left off.

chapter two

Joseph worked for as long as the daylight allowed putting the finishing touches to a seat he had been asked to make. It was much cooler at this time of year and the evenings could be quite cold. Consequently, the physical aspects of carpentry were much easier than during the summer when it often got too hot to work. But with the shortest days of the year coming this week, he knew he would have to finish work a little earlier than he would have liked. As with all things in life, there was one advantage of having an early finish; it gave him the chance to call and see Mary on the way home. Now that their engagement was official, he was allowed to visit her. So he threw his cloak over his shoulders, and set out on the short walk to her house.

It was quite chilly so he pulled his cloak a little closer to his body to keep out the effects of the wind. There was no snow on the mountains yet, but the icy wind blowing down from them indicated that snow could be building up on the highest peaks before long.

As he approached the house where Mary lived, he could hear the dulcet tones of her voice rising above all the other local sounds.

"I know she's really looking forward to getting married," he said to himself, "but she sounds even happier than usual this evening."

"Mary," he called out as he approached the door. "Come on in, my love." she immediately replied as she lowered her sewing onto her lap.

"You sound very happy this evening," Joseph said as he approached her, a smile stretching from ear to ear.

"You'll never guess what happened today, Joe." Mary said with obvious excitement.

"I have absolutely no idea," he said. "Whatever it is, it's obviously made you very happy." He moved a little closer putting his hand on her shoulder.

"I had a visitor come and see me this afternoon," she cheerfully answered with a look that said that she knew something he didn't!

"Obviously a nice visitor, judging by your reaction."

"Oh yes," Mary answered, "a very nice visitor." She teased.

"I bet my sister has been over to see you again. She's been over quite a few times since we announced our engagement," Joseph guessed.

"No, it wasn't your sister . . ." Mary paused. "It was actually someone much nicer than that!"

"I can't think of anyone nicer than my sister." Joseph replied and thought very carefully for a few moments. Then he continued, "I'm sorry Mary, but I give up! I can't think of anyone else. You'll just have to tell me who it was."

"It was an angel!" Mary exclaimed, her voice full of excitement. "I had an angel visit me!"

There was a long pause whilst Joseph considered Mary's revelation. He looked around the room as if searching for inspiration or some proof of the angelic visit, and then continued very pensively, "An angel?" he said slowly. "An angel came here?" He looked around the room again as he tried to gather his thoughts. "You're having me on, aren't you?"

Mary was so excited by her news that she had not noticed Joseph's doubtful and hesitant demeanour. "I'm not having you on," she said, still bouncing around with excitement, "an angel really did come here, and he had some very special news. And it wasn't just any angel. His name was Gabriel."

Joseph sensed that something special really had happened in the house, but he was stunned by the news. What could have happened here that could have caused this excitement. "So what was this special news the... er... angel had for you?" he asked apprehensively.

"He told me I was going to have a baby!" Mary bubbled excitedly.

"Well, that's nice to know! It would be seen as a disgrace if we got married and then had no children! It must be awful for Elizabeth, that relative of yours, and her husband. Such a shame they haven't had children, especially with him being so important in the temple." Joseph said uneasily.

"Well . . .!" Mary exclaimed. "Even that's part of my news. You see, I'm going to have a very special baby from God. And Elizabeth, the relative you were just talking about, even she's going to have a baby. In fact the angel told me she is already six months pregnant."

Joseph sat back, took a deep breath, but said nothing.

Mary continued, "I must go and see Elizabeth tomorrow to make sure she's alright. She and her husband are already quite old." She paused for breath, and then continued, "Actually I should have said that they are both too old to be having a baby, so they'll need all the help they can get."

"Just a moment," Joseph said as he reflected on the mind-shattering news he had just heard. He had to say something, so in the end he asked slowly, "If I've got this right, you're going to . . . er . . . have a baby and God is going to be his father?"

Mary nodded. "So . . . so what are you going to do?" A very troubled Joseph was already beginning to consider the implications of Mary's announcement. "I'm going to get a few things together this evening, then I'll take one of my father's donkeys and set out first thing in the morning. It's a long way to Judah." Wrapped up in her joy, Mary could not see the dangers Joseph had already seen.

"Right," Joseph said very thoughtfully, "then I'd better leave you to get on, and I suppose I'll see you when you get home again. I guess I've got some thinking and planning to do." He got to his feet, and slouched to the door, head hanging down low enough to reach his toes. "Bye, Mary," he said quietly as he went out and headed for his own home.

Mary watched his quiet, thoughtful departure. Her own level of excitement was still so high that she noticed very little of what was going on around her, and she did not recognise the doubts in Joseph's mind.

"I bet he's going to plan how to make a crib or something. He's such a nice man, and I'm so glad we're going to get married when I get back." She turned and looked around her room. "Well," she said to the empty room, "I suppose I'd better get some things sorted out, and ask my father for a donkey. Then I ought to get together everything I might need to support Elizabeth." She thought about the relatives she was about to visit, "I hope I can be of some help to them. They really are too old to be having to cope with a baby!"

Joseph walked slowly back to his own house with a heavy heart. As soon as he arrived home, he dropped onto his bed and started thinking through all the implications of today's news.

Had there really been an angel or was seeing an angel merely a ruse for Mary to hide the fact that she had been seeing someone else? This other person must have got her pregnant, but who was he? Joseph had never seen Mary with anyone else, although he was starting to realise that while he was working, he would have had no idea what she could be getting up to. Was she really pregnant, or had something only just happened? Was the angelic visitor really just another man?

"All I know is," he said to himself, "if she really is expecting a baby, then it's nothing to do with me!" He thought of all the implications for Mary. He still really loved the girl, even if she had got herself pregnant by another man. He simply could not bring himself to report her to the temple authorities.

"If I do report her," he said aloud to the empty room, "she'll be condemned and stoned to death!" The tears began to well up in his eyes as he thought of his betrothed and beloved Mary being stoned to death. He could never allow that to happen.

"There's only one solution," he said quietly. "As soon as she gets back from Elizabeth's house, I'll arrange for the engagement to be broken off, then I can send her back to live with Elizabeth and Zechariah until after the baby has been born. Doing that will give us time to consider all the options available to us. If the other man does abandon her, we could still get married. I've loved Mary for years, and I could never find anyone else like her. We'll just have to wait and see."

And with that, he cried himself to sleep.

chapter three

Mary could not understand why Joseph did not seem as happy as she was. The angel's announcement was such an amazing thing. It was just so mind-blowing that she couldn't wait to tell her wonderful news to everyone.

"Joseph must be planning something really special for the baby," she said to herself. She also couldn't understand why her mother didn't leap for joy at the news. "Just be patient, and let's see what happens," her mother had said, "and I wouldn't tell your father just yet. It's better to keep this as our secret for now, my dear!" She paused for a moment, then added, "After all, we could find it was all a dream. Or perhaps it's the result of eating something that didn't agree with you!"

Her mother knew that there were some leaves that, if accidentally added to a salad, could cause you to have strange dreams for a while. She had thought carefully about the leaves she had collected over the last few days, but she could not think of anything she may have picked that would have caused Mary to have a bad experience. "Yes, my dear," Mary's mother had continued, "it's possible I may have put a bad leaf in your breakfast and caused you to imagine the things you've told me about. So for now, I think it would be wise if you didn't tell anyone else about your visitor."

Mary could understand her mother's point of view, and she did agree with her. Indeed, it would look a bit silly if she told everyone she had been visited by an angel, and then found out later that it had been a dream. Even so, she really believed in her heart that everything had truly happened, although she had to admit her story did sound a little far-fetched.

"If my friend Rachel had come and told me that she'd been visited by an angel, would I believe her?" she said to herself. "And then if she said that she was going to have a baby, I would be asking her who she'd been lying down with." She thought about everything for a few moments, and then had a more worrying thought, "I wonder what Joseph really thinks? Does he think my visitor was all a dream, or heaven forbid, might he think I have lain down with another man! He must know I would never do that! I must make my plans to see Elizabeth! She is going to be a key person in what happens next!"

She looked around her room and considered the journey she was about to make to the town of Judah. "I must get to the market place!" she exclaimed as her thoughts began to fall into place. "I thought I saw some strangers in town today, so perhaps there's a caravan in town!"

She grabbed her shawl and set off along the narrow paths heading for the market, arriving at the same time as some travellers were settling their camels for the night.

"Excuse me," she said to the nearest man, "but are you heading south in the morning?"

"Yes, we're going south," he answered. "Why do you want to know?"

"I've got to visit a relative of mine who lives in the town of Judah." Mary replied.

The man looked as if he could be the leader of the caravan. His face was fairly weather beaten, and he looked to be in his late 40's. He drew his hand across his forehead thoughtfully. "Wow, that's a fair distance for a young lady like you. I hope you're not going to do that journey on your own?" He said. "Not running away from anything are you?"

"I am on my own, and no, I'm not running away from anything. I just need to get to a relative of mine who urgently needs my help. That's why I was hoping to join your caravan." She looked pleadingly up at the man.

"Do you have your own donkey? The journey is about 160 km, and will take us about six days." He said almost harshly as he considered the responsibility of having this youngster in tow! "Yes, I've got my own donkey," Mary replied confidently, "and I can bring my own covers and tent for the night."

"Good," the man replied firmly, "but you'll have to be here early. This time of year, we like to set out at first light, and we can't wait for you." He paused, "and it will be quite cold in the mornings." He added in an effort to discourage her.

"I'll be here!" she exclaimed. Mary knew it was an act of providence that there was a caravan passing through Nazareth that very day and even more so that it was heading south. It could be days or even weeks before another caravan came to Nazareth, heading where she wanted to go.

She rushed home and persuaded her father to let her borrow a donkey for a few days . . . or weeks so she could visit Elizabeth.

"What's so urgent that you must visit her now?" he asked sharply. "It's not the best time of the year for that journey," he continued. "Can't you wait until spring when the weather will be better?"

"No," Mary answered, "I really believe I must visit her now so that I get there before any snowfall that might be due." Then she added, "And I've just met up with a caravan going almost all the way to Judah. That will give me safety on the journey, and I should be there in five or six days."

"Doesn't Joseph mind you going?" her father challenged. He was not happy that his young, engaged daughter was about to embark on a potentially dangerous journey. She hesitated for a moment, then said, "No, he understands that I need to go." So, her father reluctantly agreed and helped her to prepare everything for the journey.

The next morning, Mary was ready very early. She loaded her things onto the donkey, and headed through the almost dark streets to the central square where the caravan had stopped overnight. Her father had deliberately selected an older, mature donkey as he was sure it would be the most reliable one.

"I really am sure all this actually happened to me," she said to herself, "but if I get to Elizabeth's and discover she isn't pregnant, then I'll know I was just dreaming. But I must find out!"

This was the first time Mary would have travelled such a long distance on her own, so she was a little apprehensive as she joined the caravan. She needn't have worried as the man she'd met in the market the previous day turned out to be very kind and reliable. He had grown-up daughters of his own and his first grandchild had been born recently. Consequently, he was very protective of young Mary, and he made sure she was not pestered by any of the other men in the caravan. He insisted on Mary riding her donkey directly behind him so that he could keep a close eye on her.

The caravan set off from Nazareth on a crisp, clear morning, and had already covered some distance before the winter sun rose. The caravan followed the foothills down towards the River Jordan. Mary looked at the rugged mountains and rocky path as the caravan made progress towards the river. She knew it would be a two-day journey to reach the river. They pressed on all day stopping briefly at mid-day before setting off again until the leader brought the caravan to a halt at dusk.

"We're camping here for the night," he announced, "as we must reach the River Jordan tomorrow."

"Why are we taking this longer route?" someone asked.

"This time of the year, I'd rather not lead a party over the hills. For one thing, you can't guarantee what the weather will be like. Also, I'm expecting to pick up some things at Beit She'an, so we don't really have any choice."

There was a sheltered area of grass nearby that caravan leaders often used for camping, and true to his word, he set up his tent in a particularly well sheltered spot and insisted that Mary put hers next to his.

The next morning he was up at the crack of dawn to get everyone organised for travelling. Mary had not slept very well, so got up as soon as she heard activity and was one of the first ready to leave.

The day was fine and sunny, and they made good progress, reaching Beit She'an late in the afternoon, where they stayed overnight before moving off along the river bank the next morning.

Travelling was now much easier and quicker. The rocky path through the mountains was replaced by a much smoother path by the river, which although quicker was quite a lot dustier. Over the following two days they travelled alongside the River Jordan most of the way to Jericho, camping on the river bank each night. Then they travelled away from the river to make a brief stop at Jericho before going on to Jerusalem.

This was the first time Mary had been to Jerusalem, and she could not get over the height of the city walls. The caravan set up camp just outside Jerusalem where the traders intended to spend a few days buying and selling produce. They offered to escort Mary to Judah a few days later when they were ready to move on.

She would have liked to spend some time looking at the famous city but Mary was very impatient to reach Judah to find out about Elizabeth's condition. This urgency outweighed her interest in staying longer, so she decided to stay with the caravan only for that night, and the next morning she said her good-byes, giving a little hug to the man who had protected her.

"I'd be far happier if you stayed with us for a few days so that we can see you safely all the way to Judah," the caravan leader said after being told about Mary's impending departure.

"I really must go as soon as possible," Mary insisted.

Eventually, the caravan leader came up with a compromise. "Look," he said, "you really remind me of my daughter, and I want to see you get there safely. I'd like to send my best man to escort you to the foothills of Judah. He'll set you on the right path, and then return to me."

"Bless you," Mary exclaimed with deep appreciation, "that is just so kind of you!" and she gave the caravan leader another hug.

The two travellers set off immediately, and true to his task, the man escorted Mary all the way to the valley leading to Judah, where she was released to complete her journey alone. Mary followed the track to Judah, and once there it didn't take her long to find Elizabeth's house.

As soon as Elizabeth saw Mary, she squealed! "Blessed are you among women, and blessed is the fruit of your womb! Blessed are you among women, and why is this granted to me that the mother of my Lord should come to me?"

"Well, I thought you'd be pleased to see me," Mary teased, "but I didn't expect you to squeal with delight! Where did all that come from?!"

"You don't understand!" a beaming Elizabeth exclaimed as she rushed forward to give Mary a long hug. "As soon as you came into the house my baby leaped . . . !"

"Your baby!" Mary interrupted. "Yes," Elizabeth continued, "my baby leaped in my womb!"

"But I didn't even know you were expecting, and how did you know that I was expecting, too? I don't even really know for certain yet!" Mary said with rising excitement.

"No . . . well, it's a long story. I'll tell you all about it later. But because of my or should I say our ages, we decided not to tell anyone about my condition yet, just in case." Elizabeth said slowly.

"In case of what?" Mary asked.

"When older ladies get pregnant, their babies are sometimes born much too early and die, so we didn't want to tell anyone just yet," Elizabeth answered. "But enough about me. Come and sit down and tell me what brought you this long distance to see us, especially at this time of the year."

Mary took her things into the house, and released the donkey into a small paddock to which Zechariah had access. She was quite tired after six days of travelling, so they did not talk much that evening, agreeing instead to swap news the next day. However, she paused before leaving everyone as she praised God and prophesied over the future.

"I'm bursting with God-news" Mary said with renewed excitement, "I'm dancing the song of my Savour God. God took one good look at me, and look what happened – I'm the most fortunate woman on earth! What God has done for me will never be forgotten, the God whose very name is holy, set apart from all others. His mercy flows in wave after wave on those who are in awe before Him. He bared His arm and showed His strength, scattered the buffing braggarts. He knocked tyrants off their high horses, pulled victims out of the mud. The starving poor sat down to a banquet; the callous rich were left out in the cold. He embraced His chosen child, Israel; He remembered and piled on the mercies, piled them high. It's exactly what He promised, beginning with Abraham and right up to now."

"Wow!" Elizabeth exclaimed. "That's a powerful statement to make just before bedtime!" Mary paused in the doorway, then turned and added, "I just felt God's hand on me." She paused, then added, "See you in the morning. Good night!" and with that she left the room.

Mary slept well, but was up as soon as she heard Elizabeth preparing breakfast.

"Now you know about my baby," Elizabeth said after breakfast, "I want to know your news! But first I must warn you, Zechariah can't talk. I'll tell you about that later."

Mary looked around the main room in Elizabeth's house. As Zechariah was an important member of the temple staff, he had a good house which, mainly due to her lack of children, Elizabeth kept looking very nice. There were several wooden seats in the room, but Elizabeth had made some cushions and covers for them. A beautifully carved wooden table sat in the middle of the room behind which Zechariah was sitting on a large wooden chair with ornately carved arms. Elizabeth sat in a similar, but less ornate chair set a little back from the table.

"Well," Mary started, "now I know your news, I really can tell you mine!" Elizabeth and Zechariah looked at Mary, both puzzled. How could their baby make a difference to Mary passing on her own news?

Zechariah waggled his finger in Mary's direction, and pointed towards an empty wooden chair which had embroidered cushions on, to which Mary went and then sat. He might not have been able to talk, but Zechariah was determined not to be totally left out of everything!

"What do you mean?" Elizabeth asked.

"Just over a week ago I had a visitor," Mary started, and then proceeded to tell Elizabeth and Zechariah about her angelic visitation. "So you see," Mary finished, "I simply had to come and see you as soon as I could. I knew you were a little too ... er ..."

"Be honest," Elizabeth chipped in, "too old to have a baby."

"Yes, but I didn't want to upset you," Mary added quickly.

"We're beyond that!" Elizabeth countered, laughing.

"I thought I could have had a bad dream and imagined the whole thing. But the angel did tell me that you were going to have a baby. If that turned out to be true, then I would know that my visitor really was who he said he was, and I would be having a baby from God. On the other hand, I also knew that if you weren't having a baby, then I must have imagined the whole thing."

"Well, that's good logic" Elizabeth said. Zechariah nodded. "And that explains something for me," Elizabeth said slowly. Mary and Zechariah looked at her. "If you remember," Elizabeth said, "when you arrived yesterday I suddenly squealed."

"I remember that!" Mary exclaimed. "My baby really did a leap in my womb. Now that I've been pregnant for over 6 months, I do feel him move sometimes, but as you came in, it felt as if I had a bucking donkey rather than a baby! And then I said that prophesy about you and your baby; until you walked in the door I didn't know you were pregnant."

Now it was Mary's turn to look for answers. "So what's been happening to you, and why can't Zechariah talk?"

"It all started six months ago when it became Zechariah's turn to serve and actually go through into the inner sanctuary. He's been serving in the temple for over forty years, and everything was right for him to be called. He got himself ready, tied the rope around his ankle as they do, and . . ."

"Tied a rope around his ankle?" Mary queried.

"Yes." Elizabeth continued, "Sometimes the power of God in the holiest place is so strong that the priest collapses on the floor after he's gone in. No-one else is allowed in, so the only way the priest can be retrieved is by pulling him out with the rope. That only happens on a few rare occasions, but my Zechariah wouldn't want to be left to die in there!"

"I'm sure he wouldn't!" Mary exclaimed sympathetically as she glanced in his direction. Zechariah shook his head vigorously, making a cutting action with his hand across his neck at the same time!

"My Zech went in, did his duties, prayed, and suddenly realised he wasn't alone!" Elizabeth continued.

"But I thought you said . . ." Mary interrupted.

"No one else was allowed in. That's right. But his visitor is someone I think you know." Elizabeth continued calmly.

"Ahhh, . . . Gabriel!" Mary exclaimed.

"That's right. And he told Zech that God really had heard our prayers for a baby and even at our age we were going to get a son we've got to raise as a Nazarite priest. He mustn't ever have his hair cut, or drink wine, and he will bring many in Israel back to YHWH." She paused for a moment, and then added, "And we've got to name him John."

"John?" Mary questioned as she looked quizzically at her relative.

"That's right. I know it's a name we have never had in our family, but that was what Gabriel said." Elizabeth answered.

"Fair enough," Mary said, nodding in agreement, "but that doesn't explain why Zechariah can't speak!"

"I think you'll have to ask him that yourself!" The two women looked at Zechariah, who sheepishly looked at the ground. "But he won't be able to answer you. You see, it was his punishment for not believing Gabriel!"

Mary smiled, "Didn't he realise who Gabriel was?"

"Oh yes he did," Elizabeth answered, "but he didn't trust God's word. So apparently, Gabriel told him that he wouldn't be able to speak again until after the child was born!"

"So that's not for another three months!" Mary stated. "That's right! I've had just over six months so far with him being unable to argue with me over anything, and I've still got almost three months to go!" Elizabeth smiled.

"Are you enjoying the peace?!" Mary teased as she looked at Zachariah, giving him a cheeky smile.

"Actually, no I'm not!" Elizabeth answered lovingly, "We don't ever argue normally, and although I enjoyed the peace for a day or so, after that it was too quiet! I wanted someone to talk to, so having you here is a real bonus."

Mary had not intended to stay with Elizabeth for very long, but on realising how much she appreciated having company, she decided to stay for at least a few weeks.

chapter four

Mary quickly settled into helping Elizabeth as she had originally intended, and now that Elizabeth's 'bump' was big enough to have started becoming a nuisance it was really appreciated. Mary could also do many of the general tasks that Elizabeth would normally have done, allowing her relative to spend more time with her legs raised, resting on a bench.

The next few weeks passed quickly, and the time soon arrived for Elizabeth to give birth. Mary sent for the local midwife, and prepared water and cloths ready for the delivery. Zechariah paced up and down outside, doing his best to wear a new path around the house as he was anxious both for his elderly wife and for his baby boy.

Mary quietly supported Elizabeth, holding her hand during every contraction, and mopping her brow afterwards. The contractions became increasingly frequent, until the time came for the delivery. Elizabeth cried out once more, and the midwife told her to push, and suddenly, there he was: the promised baby boy that Elizabeth and Zechariah had been praying for. The midwife took the baby, cleaned him with the cloths and warm water, and then wrapped him in a soft blanket, whilst Mary took care of Elizabeth.

After a few moments, the baby cried out and the midwife said everything was alright. She gave the baby to his mother, and Elizabeth lay back to rest and to let the baby suckle. Only then Zechariah was invited in to see his baby boy.

The next few days were spent with Elizabeth resting and recovering from the birth. Mary looked after the baby whenever Elizabeth needed a sleep. She also made food for everyone and started to prepare everything for her return to Nazareth. By now, spring had come, and Elizabeth was well on the way to recovery after delivering her child. Mary had no excuse to stay any longer, although she did promise she would stay until after the important eighth day.

Eight days after the baby's birth, everyone had made the required preparations and the priest had been arranged for the circumcision ceremony. Close friends and relatives started to gather at Zechariah's house, all very keen to see this amazing child.

"Shall I let them in?" Mary asked.

"Yes," Elizabeth answered. Mary looked at Zechariah for confirmation. He nodded.

"Come on in everyone," Mary said to the gathering guests. "Elizabeth and the baby are ready." All the visitors squeezed into the main room and gathered around the chair Elizabeth was sitting in, the baby asleep on her lap. The visitors gazed down at the baby, lying peacefully unaware of the trauma he was about to go through.

It is traditional for boys to have a brit milah or bris ceremony on the eighth day after their birth, in which the fore-skin is removed. The operation is conducted by an officer from the synagogue called a mohel, and he is assisted by the sandek, whose job it is to hold the baby still whilst the operation is done.

"You're lucky getting a baby at your age," one lady commented enviously. She was a few years younger than Elizabeth and she was obviously hankering for a child of her own.

"Not lucky," Elizabeth retorted. "It's all part of God's amazing plan!"

"Little Zech will be a real hit with the girls," an attractive younger lady observed. "He's got a nose just like his father!"

"Can I hold little Zechariah?" the older lady asked.

"You may hold him," Elizabeth answered, "but his name is John!"

"Zechariah-John. That's an interesting combination. It actually sounds quite good." The older lady presumed.

The younger lady immediately told everyone very loudly that she had known the family for years, and that she was actually a close relative on Zechariah's side of the family, and that, "There has never been anyone called John in the family, and I can't see why there would be!" she said with inferred authority. "And anyway," she continued, "oldest boys always take on the name of their father, so he's got to be called Zechariah!"

"Enough, Naomi!" Elizabeth chipped in sharply. "His name will be John!"

"That's not going to work," Naomi countered. "Ask his father. He's bound to call him Zechariah. Aren't you, Zech?" she said, turning to Zechariah. "Oh sorry, you can't speak can you? Give him a board and some chalk so he can write the baby's name according to tradition, as the head of the house!"

Everyone looked around the room for the board and chalk, not noticing that Zechariah had both of them on the floor beside him. He bent down, picked them up, wrote on the board and turned it around for everyone to see. On it, he had written just one word: 'John'!

"But . . . but you've written 'John' on the board!" Naomi exclaimed.

"John!" Zechariah exclaimed loudly. "His name will be John!"

Before anyone had the chance to say anything, Zechariah received a blessing in prophesy from the Holy Spirit, and proclaimed "Blessed be the Lord, the God of Israel; He came and set His people free. He set the power of salvation in the centre of our lives, and in the very house of David His servant, just as He promised long ago through the preaching of His holy prophets: deliverance from our enemies and every hateful hand; mercy to our fathers, as He remembers to do what He said He'd do, what He swore to our father Abraham –

a clean rescue from the enemy camp, so we can worship Him without a care in the world, made holy before Him as long as we live. And you, my child," he stooped down and picked up the baby, "You, my child, Prophet of the Highest, will go ahead of the Master to prepare His ways, present the offer of salvation to His people, the forgiveness of their sins. Through the heartfelt mercies of our God, God's Sunrise will break in upon us, shining on those in the darkness, those sitting in the shadow of death, then showing us the way, one foot at a time, down the path of peace." Then he sat down, and passed the baby John to the priest.

"Wow!" Elizabeth exclaimed. "Where did that come from?"

The mohel picked up the baby and handed him to the sandek who held him very still whilst the cut was made. There was a sudden scream from the baby as the operation was completed. The ladies all looked away whilst the cut was covered before resuming their conversation as if nothing had happened. The mohel handed the baby back to Elizabeth, who quickly stopped the cries in ways only a mother can.

"That's put me in my place!" a subdued Naomi said, quietly.

The next few days passed quickly with Mary helping Elizabeth as much as she could whilst Elizabeth gained strength. John was a typical baby boy, greedily feeding at every opportunity, and producing the usual baby smells and eruptions at both ends!

Zechariah happily returned to his work at the temple where everyone wanted to know how he felt. He was happily talking more than ever as if trying to catch up on all that he had missed out on during his nine months of silence . . . and Mary brooded!

She knew she must go back to Nazareth sooner or later, but how could she face Joseph? Would he believe what had happened to her or would he think she had been with another man? Would her parents understand? Should she continue to stay with Elizabeth and Zechariah? Worst possible scenario, could Joseph have reported her pregnancy to the temple officials, in which case she would be going home to die a very painful death. Eventually, she realised she really did have to go back to Nazareth.

"As soon as John is strong enough to travel, I'll come and visit you, and explain to everyone there what happened to me. I'll also write to your father and explain what I can. That may help your return," Elizabeth volunteered.

"Thank you, Elizabeth," Mary answered, "that could be very helpful."

"I was in Jerusalem earlier today," Zechariah said as he joined in the conversation, "and there was a caravan getting ready to set off for the north the day after tomorrow. The weather looks good, why don't you join it?"

"Yes," Mary answered firmly. "I must face up to returning to Nazareth, and I suppose now would be as good a time as any."

"I was hoping you'd say that." Zechariah answered. "The caravan is actually going all the way north to Tyre, and it will stop at Nazareth on the way. It could be some time before there's another one following that route, so I hope you don't mind, but I spoke to the leader and told him you would probably be joining him."

Mary pursed her lips. She had been putting off her return, but she knew she could not delay for too much longer. "Thank you," she answered reluctantly. "If I go to Jerusalem tomorrow, I'll be ready for an early departure the next day."

"I'll come with you," Zechariah said helpfully. "I've made arrangements for you to stay with one of the temple officials tomorrow night. Then you'll be ready to set off early the following morning."

The next morning, Mary said her goodbyes to Elizabeth. The two hugged lovingly, both shedding a few tears, both wondering if they would ever see each other again, then Mary and Zechariah set off, travelling down the track to head along the valley and start the long climb up to Jerusalem. Mary was on her father's donkey again, and Zechariah rode one of the young donkeys he was trying to train.

Overnight rain had settled any dust there may have been, leaving a nice fresh spring morning. If Mary had not been worrying about the reception she anticipated when she got home, she might have been able to enjoy the ride down the pass and the climb up to Jerusalem. She had been impressed by the imposing city walls and the narrow streets which were just a muddle of people that seemed to be dashing everywhere. Mary was led to a small house near the temple where she was introduced to a very warm, motherly lady who immediately put a comforting arm around her shoulders, and guided her into the house. Zechariah took Mary's donkey to the yard just behind the house where he tied its halter to a post.

"If you'd like to settle down, I'll bring a drink in for you in a moment." The house owner said lovingly. "I think Zechariah has tethered your donkey in the yard." She paused, "Oh, and I don't expect Zechariah thought to tell you, but my name's Sarah. Men often don't think about introductions, and Zechariah's still quite excited about his new arrival!"

"Thank you very much," Mary answered as she settled down on the narrow bed.

"Will you want to look around the city while you're here?" Sarah asked.

"I may have a little look around this area," Mary answered, "but I don't want to tire myself before setting out early tomorrow."

"Very wise," her host answered. "But you must go and have a look at our famous wall, and the temple."

"I've heard about the wall," Mary answered. "The Ha-Kotel or something, isn't it?"

"That's right, although it has several names already. Ha-Kotel Ha-Ma'aravi seems to be its official name. You must go and see it." Sarah insisted.

"Has it been finished now?" Mary asked, trying her best to sound interested. "Part was finished about . . . let me see," she thought for a moment, "yes, it must be about sixteen or seventeen years ago."

"So it's not finished yet then?" Mary questioned feigning interest.

"Not quite. You might be able to see the tunnels they've built. There's supposed to be a small synagogue in the tunnels, but I've never been down there." Sarah enthused.

"I'll see," Mary answered, "but I'm not going to walk very far, and I'm certainly not going down any tunnels!" She did her best to sound enthusiastic, but she really had too much on her mind to worry about any wall other than the one she imagined had now been built between Joseph and herself.

That afternoon, Mary did have a little look around Jerusalem. She was fascinated by the long narrow streets in the main part of the city, and the steep hills on which the city was built. She did walk to the Ha-Kotel, but was quite happy to look at the enormous wall from a distance. She had no intention of going down any tunnels, no matter what was at the end of them, or of climbing up to the temple.

Her favourite spot was sitting on the very wide stone steps that lead up to the temple. They were so much wider than any other steps she had ever seen. From there she could look over the valley to a large copse of young olive trees. She watched the clouds drifting over the hills for a while, and then she returned to her host so she could get a good night's rest before starting on her journey the next day.

chapter five

Mary had made all the right preparations for the journey, and she was ready in very good time. You would have expected her to be excited at going home after three months away. But anyone seeing her would have thought she was going back to Nazareth for a funeral! If ever you wanted to find a reluctant traveller, it would be Mary!

The caravan leader had very kindly taken Mary under his wing as soon as he met her. "You keep your donkey close to me on the journey," he insisted, "and make sure you sleep close to my tent. If you cry out in the night, then I'll be sure to hear you!"

Mary was very grateful for this attention, but it did little to lift her spirits. Unlike the others in the caravan, Mary paid little attention to the effects of spring on the mountains, the rising spring temperatures, and the beauty of the pass which lead to her home. All too soon, the caravan was climbing up the hill towards Nazareth.

There were always people looking out from the town, so an approaching caravan would be spotted some time before it arrived. Some of the towns people would go to the market square, anticipating what the caravan might be carrying, and at this time of the year they would be seeking fresh spring crops from the lower land where they grew earlier than on the hills, or they could be preparing to take goods that they had been making to sell to the caravan leaders. Naturally, with journeys taking as long as they did they would also be looking out for returning friends and relatives.

"Oh look!" someone shouted out as the caravan approached the city gate. "Mary's come home again! Quickly, go and tell Joseph. He'll want to know she's back so he can meet her in the square!" Some children ran off in the direction of Joseph's workshop, and Mary started wishing that she had stayed with her relatives.

"What will he say when he sees me?" she wondered. "Will he even bother to come to the caravan?" Suddenly, there he was! He was smiling. He held out his arms to her, and she ran straight into his embrace!

"You're happy to see me!" she exclaimed with some surprise. "Of course I am," Joseph answered lovingly. "And I'm sorry I didn't believe you before."

"But you do believe me now?" Mary asked.

"Yes! Only last night an angel from YHWH appeared to me in a dream. He told me that God had given you the baby, so I don't need to divorce you. He told me that I should take you home as my wife, and our child must be called Jesus." He pulled Mary close to himself again, then he turned her so they could walk back to his home side by side.

"That's the name Gabriel told me we should call him!" Mary said as they started walking.

"He also told me that He will save His people from their sins, whatever that means," Joseph continued.

"Gabriel told me something like that too," Mary agreed, "but I guess we'll just have to wait and see what happens."

"You can come to my house, can't you? Oh sorry, I'm rushing you. You must want to go and see your family first!" Joseph gushed.

An excited Mary danced off "Won't be long!" she called looking over her shoulder. "Will you organise everything?"

"Speed is essential," he replied. "We'll be married by tonight!" With that Joseph set off to organise everything that needed to be done for the wedding.

Unfortunately, a number of people overheard this conversation about the baby Jesus. Some of them did not believe or understand the divinity of Jesus, so it did not take long for them to put two and two together and presume that Jesus had been conceived illegitimately; a lie that would be thrown at him later in his life.

After the marriage, Mary moved in to live with Joseph. As every prospective mum will tell you, life carries on as usual at first. But as the baby's due date draws closer, time seems to slow down and this applied to Mary just as much as anyone else. She started to feel very unsettled, and she just wanted the next few weeks to disappear. Joseph quietly carried on with his work, although whenever he had some spare time, he put it to good use by making things for the baby. But then came the Roman Emperor's decree!

One day when Joseph was quietly working on a stool for a customer, he sensed Mary was standing in the door way of his workshop. "What are you doing here?" he asked, "You should be at home resting."

"I know," Mary answered, "But I wanted to ask you something." She paused whilst Joseph put down his saw and turned to face her. "Have you seen the decree that's been posted in the square?" Mary asked as soon as she had Joseph's attention.

"No, what's it about?" Joseph asked.

"It seems that Caesar Augustus has decided that there should be a census!" Mary stated as she struggled to see the implication of the message. She was aware that a decree from Caesar was potentially important.

"When?" Joseph asked with concern.

"Around the start of the new year, the first of Tishri." Mary replied with little enthusiasm.

"Does it say when the registration can start?" Joseph asked.

"Yes it does. Apparently you can register around the end of Elul, but why?" Mary questioned.

"I will have to register in my birthplace, which is Bethlehem and as my wife, you'll have to do the same." Joseph thought for a moment. "I've just had an idea!" he exclaimed. "Bethlehem is not that far from Jerusalem.

I wonder if we might be able to go to Jerusalem for Rosh Hashanah."

"Oh, of course. The Feast of Trumpets!" Mary agreed.

"And it's only about 10 km to Jerusalem from Bethlehem. We could possibly make the journey after we've registered." Joseph's excitement was obvious. Rosh Hashanah, the most holy day in the Jewish calendar.

Mary stood, "Look at me, Joseph!"

"I am looking, and you look beautiful!" he flattered.

She turned sideways to her husband "Now look again!"

"Point taken!" Joseph said thoughtfully, "If you feel up to the journey, we can go on to Jerusalem after we've registered. If not, we could go on a day or so later." Joseph was a little sad. To be in Jerusalem for the feast of trumpets would have been special.

"Baby Jesus seems to be getting very active these days. I wonder when he'll be born," Mary said thoughtfully as she sat down again.

"Do you remember when Gabriel paid you a visit?" Joseph asked.

"Not exactly," Mary replied, "but it was around the time of the solstice, so it would have been towards the end of Chisleu."

"That's what worries me!" Joseph remarked. "We obviously don't know when God made you pregnant, but if we add on 270 days, it means Jesus could be born around Rosh Hashanah."

"Wow," she exclaimed, with absolutely no enthusiasm. "So I'm going to be bouncing around on a donkey for a few days in late pregnancy!"

"We'll set out really early, and take a slow journey," Joseph said sympathetically.

"Why does the Emperor need a census now? Bit of a daft time to plan one!" Mary challenged.

"It's only a daft time for us," Joseph answered. "It's actually a very sensible time."

"Sensible? How do you make that out?" Mary questioned.

"If the census were to be held in the winter, it could be too cold for some people to travel, so they wouldn't go. Spring wouldn't be too bad, but all the sheep will have just given birth, so none of the shepherds would go. They'd never leave their new born lambs for any census. In the summer, it's much too hot to travel any distance. So that just leaves the autumn." Joseph reasoned.

"I see what you mean." Mary said thoughtfully.

"And also," Joseph continued, "you know what officials are like. New year, new start and all that. The start of the civil year is the first of Tishri!"

"Oh well, I guess we can't avoid it!" Mary reflected. "So how long should we allow for the journey?" She sunk into her chair.

"You said that your journey in the caravans took only 5 days, but I bet you were bounced around rather a lot!" Joseph exclaimed.

Mary nodded as she remembered the rushed journeys she'd taken not so long ago.

"I think we should allow at least six days for the journey." He paused . . . "Maybe even longer so that we're not under any pressure. I'll start getting things organised, then we can set off next week."

chapter six

The events of the next few days merged into a blur of activity. Joseph was busy organising the things they needed to take. Mary was trying to be helpful but generally finding life just a bit too hectic for her state of advanced pregnancy. But at long last, they were ready.

"We set off tomorrow morning," Joseph announced a few days later. "I want to make an early start so that we can try to get most of the way to the River Jordan before we have to stop for the night. That way, we should have easy access to water and we should be able to reach the river the next day."

Mary had a fitful night. Waking one moment because she was worried about the length of the journey in her condition. Then waking again the next moment because she just could not imagine five days riding on a donkey. Then the next time she woke, she was worrying about Joseph. She knew his donkey was going to be carrying some food, a simple tent and blankets. Would

Joseph manage to get a ride as well, or would he end up walking most of the way? Eventually, the final time she woke, she noticed that the sky was beginning to lighten.

"Joseph, Joseph," she called out quietly, "are you awake?" There was no answer, so she sat up in bed and looked for him, but he wasn't there. Then she realised there was someone moving around outside their house.

"Joseph," she called out again as she rose from their bed in the early morning light.

"It's alright, my love," Joseph answered from the darkness at the side of the house, "I've got the donkeys ready, so we can set off as soon as you're ready."

Mary was up and dressed in minutes, choosing to wear some simple, plain clothes, before poking her head out through the door. "Breakfast in five minutes," she called out to her husband and turned back into the house to get the meal ready. She re-emerged about ten minutes later and passed Joseph a basket of food that she had partly prepared the previous evening, ready for the trip.

"Breakfast time, my dear," she announced.

"Lovely, I'm just about ready for that," Joseph answered as he sat down on the bench outside their house. Mary handed her husband a plate of bread and fruit before sitting down next to him.

They ate in silence as they each contemplated the journey they would be undertaking over the next few days. "That was lovely," Joseph said as he finished. "Now I think we're ready to leave."

"Will everything be alright?" Mary asked.

"Of course it will," Joseph answered. "It's God's baby, so we can rely on Him looking after both of you!"

"That's not what I meant," Mary retorted. "I was just looking around at everything here."

"Nothing to worry about," Joseph said, confidently. "We should only be away for two or three weeks, and Abba is still a very capable carpenter. He can quietly work away on the things in the workshop. After all, it did belong to him in the past!"

"Good point! I bet he will enjoy having his workshop to himself for a few weeks!" Mary thought about her father in law and imagined him suddenly finding himself in charge of the carpenters shop again. She smiled, she knew he would enjoy the opportunity of being his own boss again for a short while.

"Okay, my dear?" Joseph took Mary by the hand and led her to a wooden mounting block he had placed beside her donkey. "Up you get. Steady now, you've got another passenger to think about!"

"But you just said God would look after us!" Mary said slightly mockingly, and with a wry smile.

"I know," Joseph laughed "but that doesn't mean that we don't have to be careful!" He settled Mary onto the thick pile of blankets he had put on the donkey's back in an effort to make the journey as comfortable as possible.

The sky was lightening by the time they left, the sun already rising brightly in the east. An almost cloudless sky indicated that the cool of the night would soon be replaced by a very warm spring day.

"Ready now?" he asked. Mary nodded, so Joseph collected the halters fastened around the heads of the donkeys and set off at a fairly brisk pace.

"Take it easy, Joe," Mary called out, "I don't want you wearing yourself out before we're halfway there."

"Don't worry, my love," Joseph called out over his shoulder. "Down the hill towards the river is the longest stretch that I want to do in one day. But I really do want to get as close to the river as I can before it's dark!"

"Well, you be careful!" Mary said sharply, knowing full well that what she said would not make any real difference. If Joseph had set his mind on achieving something, he would do his very best to succeed, no matter what she said!

The road running towards the river was quite uneven in places, and Joseph often had to slow down to pass a particularly rocky part. But as soon as they were beyond the uneven part of the track, he upped his pace again, stopping occasionally to see how Mary was coping and to water the donkeys when they came to a stream. They maintained a good pace until dusk fell, then he finally stopped to put up a little shelter for Mary and himself.

"Pity there isn't a moon tonight," Mary observed as the darkness surrounded them.

Joseph lit a candle, and settled her down as comfortably as possible. "Wrong time of the month," he answered. "The full moon was almost a week ago and it is on the wane at the moment. There will still be quite a bit of light from the moon, although it won't rise for a while yet. The early morning should be quite bright, so if you're up to it, we can make an early start again."

"I'll be ready," Mary answered. "I don't expect I'll get too much sleep tonight!"

Mary started to get some food ready for them both, whilst Joseph watered and tethered the donkeys. Joseph returned to their little camp a few minutes later. "I'm glad we got this far!" he said as he entered their little camp. "I didn't honestly expect to get this close to the River Jordan on the first day."

"I'm not surprised," Mary answered. "I could see that reaching here was your target, and I think you would have run with the donkeys if we'd been behind schedule."

They both slept well, and were up and on their way again early the next morning.

Joseph did not set quite such a fast pace this time. His aim had been to reach the River Jordan during the second day, a target that he achieved by mid-afternoon, helped by his being able to ride part of the way.

The river was beautiful, and the ground was now sufficiently level that it was quite easy to find a camping place for the night.

Mary found a log to sit on whilst Joseph unloaded and cared for the donkeys before settling them for the night. Then he and Mary found a comfortable place to sit down.

"We made good time again today, so I am going to ride part of the way again tomorrow," Joseph said as he stretched out his legs.

"I should think you are going to ride!" Mary answered. "We both said that God would be looking after us, so we just have to trust Him and His plan!"

"You're right of course," Joseph answered, as they both munched their way through some rolls that Mary had prepared. Joseph then erected their little tent, putting their things into it.

Later, they sat watching the reflection of the waning moon as it began to rise over the Jordan.

"It's very beautiful here," Mary said thoughtfully as she watched the reflections bouncing off the ripples of the flowing river.

"Could be quite a nice place to live," Joseph answered, taking Mary's hand in his. "But not very practical."

"Why not?" She answered. "It looks perfect!"

"The river is beautiful, especially at times like this. But when it's in flood, the river can be much, much wider, and up to 3 or even 4 cubits deeper [1.4m to 1.8m]. You also get bandits in areas like this!"

"Shouldn't we keep moving then?"

"Shhh!" Joseph suddenly said. "Noises! I think people are coming!"

They waited quietly, watching out in case Joseph really had heard bandits. After a few anxious moments, the noises turned out to be from a group of travellers appearing from further along the bank of the River Jordan.

"Hello," Joseph greeted the new arrivals. The leader climbed down from his camel, and greeted Joseph.

"We've followed the river from Lake Kinnerat, (also know as The Sea of Galilee) with a few people from Capernaum. Where are you from?"

"Nazareth," Joseph answered, "and we're going to Bethlehem for the Census."

"Nazareth to Bethlehem!" the leader exclaimed, "The best route for you would have been over the hills!"

"That would have been the shortest route," Joseph answered, "but my wife is expecting a child. This route may be longer, but it's much smoother and less uncomfortable for her if we follow the river bank."

"Can't argue with that," the leader answered. "I have a few in this group who are going to Bethlehem, but most are going to Jerusalem. You'd be much safer travelling with us."

"I'm sure we would be" Joseph answered with relief. "Thank you. If we can join you in the morning, we'd both be very grateful."

"You're more than welcome," the leader answered. "We'll leave early, but we have several children with us so we won't be rushing."

"That's fine," Joseph answered, "I'll go and tell my wife. She'll be so happy."

Indeed, Mary was very pleased to find they could join a caravan for the rest of the journey. "I said I couldn't understand how we'd managed to go so far today. My target distance was actually quite unrealistic, but I just felt we had to reach the river by tonight."

"And now we know why!" Mary said quietly. "We have an appointment to keep in Bethlehem."

"And possibly another appointment in Jerusalem, a day or so later," Joseph added. Mary nodded, but said nothing.

chapter seven

The next few days passed without incident. The speed of travel was much more relaxed and enjoyable, especially with the company they had from the other travellers, who were all very friendly. It was also fun having children running about during the day time and the evenings were spent chatting around a fire.

After a few more days they left the banks of the Jordan, and started along the rougher track past Jericho where they spent a night, before heading for the valley between Kfar Adumim and Ma'ale Adumim. After a good night's sleep the caravan stopped mid-morning as it reached the foothills leading up to Jerusalem.

"We are going up to Jerusalem," the caravan leader announced. "For those of you who have to register in Bethlehem, you need to take that track over there" pointing to a separate track, "It should only take you about four hours. You will be there well before dark.

May the God of Abraham, Isaac and Jacob bless you on this last part of your journey."

Joseph, Mary and a small group of travellers headed off down the track for the last part of their journey. As dusk was approaching, they arrived in Bethlehem went in different ways so that each member of the group could look for their own accommodation.

Joseph and Mary started their search for lodgings, which proved fruitless. Every spare bed in Bethlehem had been taken by others who were also there to pay their taxes. Joseph was becoming increasingly depressed as he failed to find a distant relative who could put them up. Every hotel bed was occupied and the prospect of sleeping in the fields was becoming more and more likely.

Eventually, he pleaded with one particular innkeeper, "Please, please have you anywhere we can stay? You can see my wife over there. She is due to have a baby at any time, and I must find somewhere for her to lie down."

"Well . . ." he said thoughtfully. Then he looked closely at Joseph and observed, "You look familiar, aren't you the son of Jacob? If you're not, you do look just like him."

"Yes, I am," Joseph answered. "Jacob is my father."

"So that means you are a descendent of David?" the inn keeper observed. "Yes," Joseph answered, "and I'm here with my wife who is also a direct descendent of David."

"And she is clearly due to give birth very soon," the inn keeper observed. "That makes your accommodation problem very easy to solve. You'll have to stay in the Migdal Eder, the royal compound for shepherds."

"You mean in the watchtower?" Joseph questioned. "Yes, that's right," the innkeeper answered. "As you know, the temple lambs are bred in this area and all the lambing finished a month or so ago. We've been cleaning the Tower, so that any perfect new born lambs can be kept in spotless conditions. We've already put in fresh hay and straw just in case we get a late perfect lamb. You know, they are the special sacrificial lambs that the temple needs?"

"If the room is good enough for the temple lambs, I'm sure it will be good enough for us. Please may we stay in it?" Joseph asked hopefully.

"Of course you can, but you won't put your donkeys in there, will you?!" The inn keeper stated.

"Certainly not!" Joseph replied indignantly. "I know the importance that the temple places on the purity of its perfect sacrificial lambs!"

Joseph was taken by the innkeeper to inspect the tower in case he needed to put any additional hay inside. Joseph expected to see a well built and well maintained tower, and he was not disappointed. The tower was built of well-dressed stone, and had a low doorway which he had to bend down slightly to get in through. There was a small window in the wall opposite the door way guaranteeing a flow of fresh air. Nice fresh straw lay on the ground and there was a stone manger built into the wall. A good stock of fresh hay had been neatly stacked against the side wall as if the room had been expecting them. A wooden door had been made on the inside of the tower so that any lamb put in the tower could not accidentally escape.

Joseph smiled a very satisfied smile and muttered to himself, "Just perfect." He looked back to the tower as he left and realised it also had an outside stone staircase leading up to the roof on which a wooden shelter had been built with a roof made from rushes.

Joseph went to collect Mary, and led her to the Migdal Eder. "Wow!" she exclaimed, "it's almost like a small palace!"

"Do you think you will be comfortable here?" Joseph asked lovingly.

"Of course I will," Mary answered, "and while you were looking at the tower the inn keeper's wife came to see me and has promised any food, blankets or supplies we might need."

As dusk was falling fast, Mary and Joseph tied up their donkeys, and Joseph carried their belongings, and the last of the food into the tower. He closed the door and then the two finished the last of their food before settling down for the night.

The next morning, both Mary and Joseph overslept after all the travelling. Joseph was up first he and went to the inn to buy some supplies for breakfast, which he took back to the tower.

"Will you be looking for anywhere else to stay?" Mary asked after breakfast.

"No," Joseph answered, "This feels right for some reason."

"I was hoping you'd say that," Mary replied. "I would never have expected to feel settled in a sheepfold. But like you said, it feels exactly right, for some reason."

"And it isn't just any sheepfold," Joseph added. "Only perfect lambs are allowed in here."

"Only the best for our little lambkin." Mary said lovingly.

"You're not expecting him to be born here are you?" Joseph contemplated Mary's first child, and the Son of God being born in a humble sheep fold.

"I don't know," Mary answered thoughtfully, "but he does seem to be pushing against me a lot at the moment."

"Probably reacting to the journey!" Joseph added sympathetically.

"We shall have to wait and see!" Mary paused . . . "I suppose we'll have to pay our taxes and register today, won't we?"

"Yes," Joseph answered. "Register first thing and then get some supplies and relax for the rest of the day so we can try to get to Jerusalem for Rosh Hashanah tomorrow."

"How far is it from here?" Mary asked.

"It's about two hours walk each way, so we could go in the morning, and come back here in the evening, if we wanted to." He paused . . . "Or we could even stay overnight to save you doing both journeys on the same day," Joseph added thoughtfully.

"We'll see," Mary said pensively, "but I'm not sure about staying overnight!"

"Why not?" Joseph asked.

"If Bethlehem was fully booked because of the census, how much fuller will Jerusalem be?" Mary answered wisely.

As Bethlehem was the place of Joseph's birth, a number of people stopped him as he looked very much like his father, Jacob. He chatted to several who thought they might know him. Mary found these stops a little embarrassing as they asked the inevitable questions. When is the baby due and when did you get married?

"Do you have to talk to absolutely everyone?!" she asked at one point.

"The alternative is to be rude and ignore them. How would that look?" Joseph said firmly.

"Point taken!" Mary reflected, "Still, I suppose this won't go on for ever. Jesus has got to come sometime soon, then everyone will forget my condition, and just go 'gaga' over the baby."

They started to walk back towards the tower when Mary suddenly stopped and grabbed Joseph's arm.

"You alright?" he questioned.

"Sharp pain!" Mary exclaimed. "I don't think Jesus is going to wait much longer."

"We'd better get back to the sheepfold," Joseph said as he supported his wife. The two made slow progress, but finally, after several more twinges of pain, they arrived back at the Migdal Eder. Mary collapsed in a heap on the fresh hay they had previously spread on the floor. Joseph went in to see if the innkeeper's wife, Ruth, had any soft blankets just in case the baby arrived.

"Ruth," he called out, "could you come and give a hand here? Seems we might be getting a baby tonight!"

The innkeeper's wife immediately sprang into action. "We've had a lot of very special newly born lambs in that room," she said, "but we've never had a baby born there. That will be something very special! Do you think it will come tonight?"

"We don't know when he will be born, but I suppose he could come tonight."

"It could be a little girl."

"He will definitely be a boy," Joseph said, "but we will need some cloths to wrap him in." Ruth gave Joseph a quizzical look. How could he be so certain it would not be a baby girl? After a short pause she continued

"We've got the swaddling cloths we wrap the perfect new-born lambs in. We're getting ready for the next lambing season, so they're all spotlessly clean."

"They'll be perfect," Joseph answered. Ruth disappeared into another room, then emerged a few moments later with some swaddling cloths in her arms.

"Here you are, and don't be afraid to give me a call if you need any help. I've helped at the birth of lots of lambs," she smiled, "and even a few babies in town."

"I'll remember that," Joseph said thankfully. "Now I must get back to Mary."

During the evening, Mary had a number of painful twinges, and she spent most of the evening holding Joseph's arm, digging her nails into him whenever there was a sudden, sharper twinge. Suddenly she cried out loudly.

"I think he's coming!" she exclaimed, panting quickly.

"Should I get some help?" Joseph asked, anticipating a quick dash to get Ruth.

"Argh!" Mary exclaimed, "Don't leave me!" Her nails dug deeply into Joseph's arm. "Get Ruth . . . get Ruth . . . Don't leave me alone!"

Joseph rushed into the inn to summon the help of the innkeeper's wife, wondering how he could call for help and not leave Mary! "He's coming, he's coming," he shouted.

Ruth was on the scene almost immediately, with clothes, swaddling cloths, water, and some soft woollen blankets. "You leave this bit to me!" she exclaimed as she entered the tower. "I know what to do at times like this, and all men do is get in the way!"

Joseph waited outside, leaning against the tower, and looking at the stars. "It's a beautiful night," he said to himself, "but I suppose we won't get into Jerusalem for Rosh Hashanah now!"

As he looked around, he heard a noise behind him. Then he heard a cry. He turned and waited and finally he saw Ruth emerging from the tower. "Congratulations!" she exclaimed, "It's a boy! Both mother and baby are doing well. You can go in again now."

"Thank you," he said, and he turned to go back into the tower. If he had waited outside just a few more seconds, he may have had a real shock, but he didn't wait! Instead, he settled back on the floor with his wife and new born baby.

Seconds later, the sky lit up over a little paddock not far from the watchtower. Angels had turned up to welcome the birth of the very special, perfect lamb, the Lamb of God!

chapter eight

Bethlehem had long been famous as the place where lambs were bred for sale at inflated prices in the temple courtyard. These lambs were kept in the enclosures close to the tower. When any lamb was born, it would immediately be gathered and thoroughly inspected. Only the lambs considered to be 'perfect' were wrapped in swaddling cloths and carefully placed in the Migdal Eder with their mother. These lambs would be kept clean and safe there until they were needed as a sacrifice by the priests at the temple in Jerusalem.

These were the most important lambs in the whole of the Jewish world. They were almost treated like royalty until they were taken by the temple officials. There was always a guard stationed at the top of the tower to keep watch and to shout or blow a warning on his shofar if he saw the sheep in any danger. The other lambs were kept in paddocks near the tower for ordinary people to buy in the temple.

Out on the lower hills around Bethlehem other shepherds would be guarding the sheep that were not to be used for sacrifice.

The night Jesus was born started like any normal night, with the shepherds chatting around a roaring log fire. As wolves were quite common they took turns walking around the sheep to check their safety. Because of this continual threat to the sheep, the shepherds needed to stay alert.

"What's that?" one suddenly exclaimed.

"It's a man! How did he get there?" a frightened shepherd queried.

"He's big! And . . . And . . . He's glowing!" another exclaimed.

"I'm not looking!" another shouted as he threw himself down on the ground so that he would not have to look at the strange apparition.

"Do not be afraid!" a calm, rich voice emanated from the glowing being. "For behold, I bring you good tidings of great joy which will be to all people. For there is born to you this day in the city of David a Saviour who is Christ the Lord. This will be the sign to you. You will find the baby wrapped in swaddling cloths and lying in a manger."

The shepherds were speechless! They looked at each other, back to the glowing man and then to the sheep to make sure they were still there! They were.

Suddenly a host of other angels appeared with the first one and they were all praising God, saying, "Glory to God in the highest, and on earth peace, goodwill toward men!"

After a short while, all the angels departed, leaving the shepherds staring silently at the vacant space the angels had previously occupied.

"Did that really happen?" one asked after a pause.

"I think so," a shepherd named Micah answered as he looked at one of his friends for confirmation. Their friend, Daniel, just stood with a puzzled look on his face, nodding.

"Did the angel actually say we had to go and find this baby?" Mishael asked.

"Yes," someone answered, "but how will we find a baby in Bethlehem? It's quite a big city, and many houses have a manger."

"That's easy!" Simon, the leader said. "What did the angel say? You will find the baby lying in swaddling cloths! That is your answer!"

"Ah, of course," Mishael said. "There is only one place where swaddling clothes are used, and that is the place where the perfect, sacrificial lambs are kept!"

"Oh yes," someone else joined in, "he's got to be in the tower!"

"Just a minute!" Micah cut in on the excitement, "we can't just leave our sheep to go on a baby hunt! Suppose a wolf comes?"

"I think if the angels told us to go, then the sheep will be safe." Simon answered, "I'm prepared to trust the angels, but if you'd like to volunteer to stay here and look after them Micah, then you're welcome to."

"If you're going Simon, then so am I!" Micah exclaimed.

The shepherds set off knowing exactly where they had to go. They quickly found Mary, Joseph and the baby, just as the angel had told them. The shepherds stayed for some time because they realised that this baby really was a very special child.

"Why is He so special?" Micah asked.

"Let me explain," Joseph answered and he then told the shepherds about Jesus.

"Wow!" Simon, exclaimed as he went back to worship the baby. He knelt down and gently stroked Jesus' cheek. "Wow!" he said again very quietly, then bent forward and kissed his forehead before standing up again.

"If we don't get back to our sheep, a wolf could attack them!" Micah said quietly, but firmly. The others agreed, so they left the family, and started to return to their flock in the fields. However, when they met anyone on the way back, they stopped and told them about the amazing things they had seen and heard.

"This has been a most amazing place for Jesus to be born," Mary said a few days after the birth, "but we can't stay here."

"God seems to have that in hand." Joseph answered with a huge smile on his face.

"What do you mean?" queried Mary.

"Ruth has been prompted to do something," Joseph said enthusiastically, "so she's persuaded her husband to let us live in a little annex they have at the side of the inn."

"That's all very good, but we can't just move in and expect them to look after us!" Mary retorted.

"Ruth has even thought of that. Apparently, there are a few carpentry jobs needed to be done at the inn. The local carpenter is very good, but he hasn't been well recently. He desperately needs a skilled carpenter to help him for a while in his workshop nearby. Looks like Ruth's got everything sorted out!" Joseph replied in awe of how things were working out.

"That's brilliant!" Mary exclaimed.

Joseph was still puzzled about one thing, "But I thought you'd want to rush back and show everyone your baby?" he said.

"Let's just say I'd be quite happy to stay here a few weeks, or even a few months first." Mary said thoughtfully.

Joseph looked at Mary, obviously puzzled by this. Every first-time mum he'd ever known couldn't wait to show off their new baby. "Are you alright, my love?" he asked.

"I'm fine," she answered. "It's just that if we go back with a baby now, people will remember when we got married. If we wait a month or two, they might have forgotten the date!"

"Oh, sorry," Joseph said thoughtfully, "I hadn't thought of that!"

"No, you're a man!" Mary said sweetly, "I wouldn't expect you to." She thought for a few moments, and then added, "There is something that does need to be done."

"What's that?" Joseph asked.

"In a few days, Jesus will be eight days old!" Mary said thoughtfully.

"You're right!" Joseph said as he considered the tasks in hand. "I'll move us into the annex in a moment, and then I've got some planning to do!"

At the same time that God sent the angel to announce the birth of Jesus to the shepherds, He also sent another angel. One that hovered like a bright light near the Babylon school of prophecy that had been started by Daniel.

chapter nine

The next few days passed by very quickly. Mary was busy looking after the baby, getting the annex the way she wanted it, and gathering together all that she needed for the next few weeks. This turned out to be much easier than she expected, as the shepherds had done quite a good job of informing people about the special birth.

Almost everyone wanted to help a baby whose arrival had been heralded by angels, so Mary eventually had to politely decline quite a lot of the gifts she was offered. Joseph had a similar problem as he tried to plan the 'brit milah'.

Going to the synagogue should have been easy, but everywhere Joseph went he was stopped by people inundating him with questions about himself and the baby. He was invited into house after house so that he could share his story, and the story of the very special baby.

"And you really are descended from David?" was usually the second or third question, followed by a similar question about Mary!

"Both of you direct descendants! Wow! That's great, but quite unusual. It's fairly common to find one parent who can trace their lineage back to King David. But both parents . . . ! I've always lived in or near to Bethlehem, and I don't know of many people who can trace both parents back to King David!" one man insisted.

"There must be some people," Joseph answered. "I can't believe Jesus is the only baby who can do that!"

"You're probably right," the man said thoughtfully, "but what about the angels and everything? I wonder . . . !"

At the synagogue, Joseph had the feeling that he had been expected as the people he needed to see seemed to be waiting for him. He made all the necessary arrangements, including the special prayers to be spoken, and for the mohel and sandek to visit Mary and Joseph's new home to perform the operation.

Eventually, Joseph returned home and told Mary what he had arranged. "They will come here on the eighth day," he said, "and obviously you can be there as your time of uncleanness will have been completed after seven days."

"I know the tradition," Mary answered, "and I know I can't touch anything during the ceremony and the naming, but I'm wondering . . ." she paused. "Have you arranged for a mohel and a sandek?"

"Of course I have," Joseph answered.

"Well," Mary said slowly, "I just wondered if you could be the sandek for the operation?" she paused, "I think it's a horrible thing to do to a baby, and I think it would be good if you were holding him rather than some stranger!"

Joseph considered Mary's request, "I have arranged for a sandek, but I'll ask the mohel when they both arrive."

So that is indeed how the ceremony was conducted. Joseph made his request when the mohel and sandek arrived the next day, and he was given permission to hold Jesus on his lap whilst the mohel put the shield in place and made the cut while naming the baby 'Jesus'.

Jesus showed His objection to the events by screaming very loudly! He was clearly most unhappy about everything, and both Mary and Joseph had tears running down their faces.

As soon as the ceremony had been completed, Mary held her arms out towards Joseph and the baby. "Can I hold Him now?" she sobbed.

"Of course you can," Joseph answered handing Jesus over to his mother. He then took the flesh that had been removed, and completed the ceremony by burying it in the ground outside the house.

By the time Joseph returned, Mary had covered the area that had been bleeding and she was cuddling a baby that was, unsurprisingly, still very unhappy with everything that had been done to him.

The next thirty-two days passed by quite quickly. Jesus recovered from the painful shock of the circumcision ceremony. Joseph settled down helping the Bethlehem carpenter. Mary marked time as she waited for the days of purification to be completed, as laid down by the law of Moses.

Forty days after the birth, she was ready for the journey to the temple in Jerusalem. Joseph was up fairly early so he could feed and water the donkeys before they set out.

The journey could have been completed in two hours, but Mary did not want to rush. The last time Mary had done this journey, enjoying the view was the last thing on her mind. This time she looked at everything they passed whilst the donkeys trudged gently towards Jerusalem. They arrived at the temple quite late in the morning and went straight to the temple market stalls so they could buy a pair of turtle doves or two young pigeons to offer as a sacrifice to the Lord God. They took the sacrifices and baby Jesus into the temple so they could present them as the law required.

As they approached the front of the temple, an old man came up to them and held out his arms so that Mary might let him hold the baby. "My name is Simeon," he said in an aged voice, "and God sent me here today because He knew you would be coming for the purification." He looked at Mary and the baby, and held his arms out again. "Please may I hold the baby?" Mary knew inside that it would be alright to pass Jesus over to Simeon.

"Of course," she said, holding Him out to the old man.

Simeon took the baby in his arms and blessed him. He hesitated for a moment as if he had been going to give Jesus back to his mother. But then he drew Jesus back to his chest and said, "God, you can now release your servant; release me in peace as You promised. With my own eyes I've seen your salvation; It's now out in the open for everyone to see: a God-revealing light to the non-Jewish nations, and of glory for your people Israel."

During the preceding six weeks, Mary and Joseph had started to become accustomed to strange things happening around them and their very special baby. But this sudden and unexpected prophesy was not what they expected to be happening in Jerusalem! Nobody here had seen the angels or the shepherds, so Mary and Joseph did not expect anything other than to be treated like two ordinary parents with a baby!

Then Simeon turned to Mary and Joseph and handed Jesus back to them. He blessed them both and then said to Mary, "Behold, this Child is destined for the fall and rising of many in Israel, and for a sign that will be spoken against, that the thoughts of many hearts may be revealed." Then looking at Mary he added, "A sword will pierce through your soul also." Then he turned and walked away as Mary shivered involuntarily.

"We were just getting used to the attention in Bethlehem and now we have potential problems in the future!" Joseph said quietly.

"It was that last part . . ." Mary said very quietly. "He directed that last comment directly at me! A sword will pierce my soul . . . !" she paused again. "If he's right, I'm not looking forward to that! I wonder what he meant."

They turned to leave the temple when an old lady hobbled up to them. She had been of average height, but now had a slight stoop. She wore a very dark, loose fitting robe, and a creased white shawl that hung on her head and draped over her shoulders.

"I praise You Lord" she said in an amazingly firm voice. "Let all who are here take note. This baby will grow, and as a man, he will be here for all seeking redemption in Israel." Then she turned and went on her way again.

"Who was that?" Joseph asked.

"I have absolutely no idea!" Mary answered. "Some sort of prophetess, I expect."

A temple worker overheard them speaking about the old lady and joined in the conversation, "Did I hear you asking about our Anna?"

"Yes," Joseph answered. "We were wondering if she was from the temple or just happened to walk in off the street as we arrived."

"Anna's a very special person," he answered. "You are right in thinking that she's a prophetess. She's prophesied here for many years . . ." He paused for a moment. "If I remember correctly, she's lived in the temple for almost sixty years. I believe she is from the tribe of Asher. Her husband died after only seven years of marriage and as she didn't have any children she moved into the temple. Actually, it must be just over sixty years ago, and she has been praying and fasting on and off here ever since. A real prayer warrior, if ever I saw one!"

"Thank you for that," Joseph said.

"You're welcome," the temple worker replied as he went back to his work.

Mary and Joseph returned to the task of completing everything they had to do before leaving Jerusalem and returning to Bethlehem.

Clouds had gathered whilst they were in the temple, and there was a possibility of rain falling. "I think we need to get moving," Joseph said firmly as they untied the donkeys. Mary mounted quickly whilst Joseph held the baby, which he passed to her as soon as she was settled. He then mounted his donkey, and they both set off on the return journey to Bethlehem. Both were lost in their thoughts, so little was said on the journey. Mary was thinking of all she had heard, and Joseph was focused on avoiding any rocks over which the donkeys could stumble. Neither noticed the clouds that were beginning to gather.

Once they had arrived in Bethlehem, Mary looked at Joseph and said, "Do we have to go back to Nazareth just yet?"

"You're really worried about the people there, aren't you?" Joseph asked quietly. Mary nodded. "If I can continue to have enough work, and the people in Bethlehem are prepared for us to stay, then that's fine. But I would like to go back quite soon, so let me know when you feel ready for the return journey."

Mary settled Jesus down for a sleep after the journey as light rain began to fall. Mary sat next to Joseph and snuggled up to him. "I will tell you Joe as soon as I feel ready to go back. Joseph, I do love you. You're so understanding." She snuggled up to her husband. Joseph smiled and gave Mary a playful kiss.

chapter ten

As evening approached, Bel-sharra looked out of the large palace window and gasped in surprise. "Hey, you three. Come and look at this."

The Magi were working in a large study room that the Magi often used for their work. It was in a particularly grand section of the Babylon palace as they were very important people in the Babylonian kingdom. Their room was at the end of a wing on the first floor of the palace and had windows opening in three directions. The larger window opened to the east so they could see the rising of the sun and other astronomical events.

Bav-il, Labashi and Nabu-naid rose from their work for the king and joined Bel-sharra at the window. "What do you make of that?" he said, pointing to an unusually bright star that seemed to be very close to Babylon. "Have you ever seen that before?"

"No!" the others exclaimed. "I think we should watch what happens to it and then we'll have to go to the library and search through the scrolls until we can find something about it."

They noted where the new star had appeared and then went back to the dream interpretation they were working on, and for which they were well-known.

"I can't settle," Labashi said after a few moments. "As you well know, I've spent a lot of time studying the stars, and I've never known a star to suddenly appear. They just don't do that!"

"Yes indeed," Nabu-naid agreed. "Your knowledge of the stars is greater than mine. I've spent much time following your example, and I've never seen a sudden appearance before . . ." He paused, looked at his three friends, and said, "I'm certain I've read in the past that a new star heralds the birth of a very significant and important king. I'm going to the library now to confirm it." He gathered the folds of his me'il [a robe for men of rank] around him, and set off for the palace library.

"I wonder if that means we will have to appoint a successor to Phraates IV sooner than we expected," Bav-il observed thoughtfully.

"Well," Labashi added, "we all know that Phraates is not popular with the people. I mean, they tried to depose him just a few years ago and now he is getting rather old."

"You could be right," Bav-il replied. "If that's what this star is about, we'd better get some of the other Magi to start a detailed search for a suitable new king, whilst we go through the library to see what we can find out about strange stars."

"Excellent idea," Labashi agreed. "When we've got everything sorted, we can then focus our efforts on whatever seems to be most important. And with that in mind, I'm off to join Nabu-naid in the library." Following Nabu-naid's example, he gathered his slightly more-flamboyant me'il around his shoulders to keep out the evening breeze, and set off.

"I'll come with you," Bav-il said, as he followed Labashi along the wide, tiled passage to the library. Once there they started to search through the many scrolls stored in the library, hoping to find something that would help explain the sudden appearance of this bright star.

Labashi spent two hours trying to find some reference without success, so he decided to re-join Bel-sharra to see if he had come to any conclusions. As he headed back towards their study he met Bel-sharra in the passageway.

"I was just coming to get you," Bel-Sharra said as the friends met.

"Why," Labashi asked. "Has something happened, or have you discovered something?"

"Neither, actually," Bel-sharra answered. "It's that new star!"

"Disappeared, has it?" Labashi joked. "No . . ." Bel-sharra hesitated looking puzzled. "It just hasn't moved!"

"But that's impossible!" Labashi said.

"I know, but come and see for yourself." Bel-sharra invited.

"One moment," Labashi said thoughtfully, "I'll get the others so they can see this as well." They both went to the library where they invited Nabu-naid and Bav-il to observe the star with them.

The four Magi went back to their study and gathered around the big window through which they had first seen the star. "So what's happened?" Labashi asked.

"See for yourself," Bel-sharra said. "But the answer is ... Nothing!" They all gathered around the window to watch this bright, new star.

"As we all know," Bel-sharra started, "the stars move around in giant circles in the sky every night. We can watch the stars and know where they were an hour ago, and we can predict where they will be one hour later."

"And they'll do exactly the same thing tomorrow night, and the next night, and so on," Bav-il added.

"Then we have the gods," Bel-sharra continued, "like Mars and Venus. They have a different path from the stars. They move on a regular path across the sky, sometimes disappearing for a while, but returning on a regular timetable."

"Yes," Labashi added. "But this star ...?"

"As you can see," Nabu-naid added, "it hasn't done anything!"

"It must be there for a reason," Bel-sharra said firmly, "so I think we should make a concerted effort to go through all the scrolls that we can access, until we find an answer."

"It's getting late now" Labashi observed. "I suggest we call it a night, and start our serious research tomorrow morning."

The wise Magi started to go towards their sleeping quarters when Bav-il happened to look up. "It's gone! That star's gone!" he exclaimed.

"Must be the cloud cover," Nabu-Naid commented, casting a quick glance at the sky.

"What cloud cover?" Bav-il observed. "All the other stars are visible."

"Perhaps it's a warning about something," Nabu-naid offered by way of an explanation.

"We'll see what we can find out tomorrow!" Bav-il commented, and with that, the four puzzled friends retired to bed.

Over the next few weeks, the Megistanes [Magi] embarked on some deep and lengthy studies. A group of Magi were appointed to try and find a suitable replacement for the King of Parthia, the old king Phraates, as this seemed to be the most likely reason for the star. All the scrolls were investigated in the library. Eventually, they came across scrolls that were five hundred years old, going back to the time of the prophet Daniel. Reading these scrolls, they began to realise that the star might not be connected with Persia. In fact, the star could have something to do with the buffer zone between Persia and the Roman Empire.

And as for the star itself, they discovered it had the very strange ability of appearing and disappearing almost at will. It seemed to spend most of the early evening hovering just to the east of where they had been working!

After a lot of research, they finally concluded that the star referred to a very important king that would be born, probably in Israel.

"There is one problem with that," Bav-il observed.

"And what's that?" Bel-sharra enquired.

"The star seems to be slightly to the east of us," Bav-il answered, "and Jerusalem is to the west."

"That's true Bav-il, but I don't know of any significant kingdoms to the east of Babylon. To the west, there is the . . . er . . . the mighty Roman Empire. And we all know what their King Herod is like!" Bel-sharra observed thoughtfully.

"I think we should mount an expedition to see what we can discover," Labashi announced. "All the pointers indicate that the king is to be a very special king. He is to be born in Israel. But I agree, it could be a king for the Roman Empire!"

"Yes," Bav-il agreed, "but if it is a Roman king, there'll be trouble!"

"That's an understatement!" Bel-sharra exclaimed. "Think of the history!"

"Oh yes," Labashi replied. "The Romans attacked Jerusalem about fifty years ago, didn't they? You're the historian, Bav-il."

"Yes, fifty-three years ago, actually, under their commander Crassus. They tried to defeat our armies, but we trounced them!" He paused for a moment . . . "Then they tried again, thirty-five years ago, under Mark Anthony."

"But our armies defeated the Romans again, didn't they?" queried Labashi.

"That's right," Bav-il continued. "But they've had a lot of trouble since."

"Something to do with King Herod, I believe," Labashi replied. "That's right," Bav-il said thoughtfully.

"The Romans appointed him as King. But he was so frightened of our forces and the unrest in Israel that he didn't manage to enter Jerusalem for another three years!"

"The Jews don't like him much, do they?" stated a thoughtful Labashi.

"They don't like him at all," Bav-il continued. "But he's not frightened of the Jews. Actually, he's frightened of us!"

"So it won't be safe for us to go there with only a small entourage?" Nabu-Naid said, more as a statement than a question.

"Positively unsafe!" Labashi answered, "If we're going to go and see this new king, we'll need nothing short of a small army. Otherwise, we'd never get out alive! He'd love to capture a few of us as prisoners or hostages!"

"How long do you think we should allow for the journey?" Nabu-naid requested, pragmatically.

Labashi thought for a few moments whilst he considered the logistics involved. "Going with a legion of soldiers, we'll be able to travel quite quickly. So we should be able to cover the distance in about two, or two and a half months. Ordinary people usually allow four months for that journey but we should be able to cover the distance much more quickly. I think we should try to get there as quickly as possible so that Herod doesn't hear about us coming before we arrive,"

"Sounds like we need to get an army together to escort us for up to - I don't know, I suppose to be safe we need to plan for as much as six months," Nabu-naid said thoughtfully. "When should we leave?"

"It can be very cold in the mountains in the winter, so I wouldn't suggest leaving during Adar or Nisan [January or early February]. Maybe leave at the end of Nisan, just a bit before the spring equinox," said Bav-il, ever the practical one!

"If he really is a very special king, then we'll have to take some very special gifts for him," Bel-sharra suggested. "Let's search through all the scrolls covering events like this, and then we must pray and ask YHWH to show us something special about this king," Bav-il commented.

The friends spent the next few weeks organising their trip. They searched the scrolls, discovering that one old scroll that suggested the possibility of a very, very special king of Israel. However, in all the scrolls, they found no recorded evidence of God actually sending a star to welcome a king. This made them realise how special this king was going to be, assuming there really was a king to be found. However, they did notice one peculiar thing.

"Have you noticed anything about the star?" Nabu-naid said one day during the month of Nisan.

"It's still there every evening isn't it?" Bav-il replied.

"Yes, but where is it in the morning?" Nabu-naid challenged.

"It usually disappears in the morning doesn't it?" Bav-il commented.

"It used to disappear in the morning, but for the last few days I've seen it in the morning, but it has been to the west of us!" Nabu-naid said.

The next day the Magi all looked to the west first thing in the morning and discovered that Nabu-naid was right. The star seemed to hover to the east in the evening, but to the west in the morning.

"Do you think it's trying to tell us something?" Bel-sharra observed when they were chatting later.

"We'll soon see!" Nabu-naid said, "But until we know more, let's just keep up with our research and get everything ready for our departure."

"I've been through dozens of prophesies about this king, and it is very strange," Bav-il announced as they started to prepare for departure.

"What do you mean?" Nabu-naid asked.

"We all agree this has to be a special king, so I was planning to take some gold. I mean, you always take gold for a king, don't you." Bav-il stated practically.

"Fine, so what's the problem?" Nabu-naid asked.

"Well," Bav-il continued, "I had planned to take a few large chests that I was going to fill with gold gifts. But I had a really powerful dream in which God showed me that we mustn't take too much!" He paused . . . "Now this is going to be a very special king, so I thought a chest of gold was probably too little. But actually, I am pretty sure that a chest would be far too much! I have arranged for some small amounts that we can use to trade for food, and a quantity of gold coins that could be carried in a saddlebag!" He paused again, as if waiting for the others to raise an objection, but none of them objected. "It's almost as if He'll be going on a journey. Very strange."

"Perhaps His life will be in danger," Labashi said thoughtfully, "because I woke up the other night and was convinced that I had to plan to take two different gifts: frankincense and myrrh! Well, we all know that those spices are very expensive, but they're not as valuable as gold. I'm wondering if our visit is as much prophetic as anything else."

"I'm sure you're right," Bav-il said. "Frankincense is a special oil that's given to priests of very high standing. If we're right, this King is going to be unique! Whoever heard of an important King also being a Priest of a very high order!"

"Actually, there has been one, but only one . . ." Everyone looked at Nabu-naid, who paused and then said, "In my research through the Hebrew scrolls, I found just one: a man named Melchizedek. He was regarded as a king and a priest."

"But the other gift," Labashi continued, "is myrrh! Now that really puzzled me because that seems to indicate a death."

"All we can do is be obedient to what we believe God has shown us," Bav-il announced. "If we can get everyone ready to leave with all the necessary supplies, we could leave in three days."

"I see no reason why not," Bel-sharra said. "The legion of soldiers is ready; the camels are organised and ready; the gifts are ready. I think we could actually leave in two days. That's just after the end of Nisan,"

"So let's do it!" Bav-il exclaimed. "We finalise everything tomorrow, and unless any of you come up with a problem, we leave at first light the following day!"

chapter eleven

"Hey, look at that!" Bel-sharra exclaimed two days later as they went out in the early morning. The sky was very clear, with not a cloud in sight. The desert air was almost cold, as usual for this time of year. And the star was out in front of them! "What do you make of that?"

"The star looks slightly brighter than before, but otherwise, everything looks as I would expect," Labashi replied as he gave the star a casual look.

"Yes, but where is the star?" Bel-sharra asked.

"It seems to be in its new morning position, just a little in front of us," Labashi replied thoughtfully. "But up until today, it has always seemed to rise in the east, and then very recently hover slightly to the west in the morning! Did anyone see it last night?"

Everyone looked at the star. "I didn't see it rise last night because I was making final preparations for the journey." Nabu-naid observed.

"But I did!" Bav-il exclaimed. "I meant to draw your attention to it last night but with all the preparations going on, sorry, I forgot! But, I did see it last night, and I saw it in the west! But now it's not due west of us, it's slightly to the north-west of us!" Bav-il was now quite excited.

"That's exactly the direction we need to go," Nabu-naid observed as he carefully scanned the sky.

"I think we will have to pay careful attention to the star on our journey," Bel-sharra observed. "We could be in for a few surprises!"

Although the Magi were in charge of the expedition, the legion's commanding officer was in charge of the management of the journey. He rode his young and very fit camel around the complete force inspecting everything before heading back to the front.

"Everyone ready?" he shouted as he turned to face the expedition. He turned around again, raised his arm and then lowered the straight arm until it was pointing forward. That was the signal for the troop to start; and it did.

With two months of travelling ahead they set off at a good, steady pace so that they did not over-tire the camels which had been well-watered and fed during the previous days in preparation for their arduous journey.

Some of the soldiers carried swords and shields while riding very sleek young camels with lightweight saddles. Other soldiers were mounted on fighting horses that had been trained for battle conditions, in case they were confronted by a Roman legion during their travels. The Magi had mature, strong camels with lavish saddles and saddle cloths. The harnesses were ornate and heavily decorated, signifying the importance of their riders. Saddlebags carried the gifts the Magi had gathered together for the new king. They also carried additional clothes that the Magi might need. There were also some supply camels carrying a large quantity of food.

The next twenty days were much the same as each other. The troop headed in a north-westerly direction, following the course of the River Euphrates. The Magi were very fit, but they did not have the training of the soldiers. Consequently, the pace was slightly slower than an army on manoeuvres, although they still made very good time. The daily programme amounted to everyone getting up at the very first touch of daylight for breakfast, then the minimalistic camp was demolished at high speed, and everyone mounted their animal ready to depart. The camp was always made by a stream so water was available. In the interest of speed, there were the minimum number of stops during the day, and the expedition kept going until daylight faded.

During this part of the journey the travellers had the River Euphrates on one side, with occasional bushes, trees and little settlements where the ground was more fertile. On the other side the mountains were bare and stark with occasional patches of scrub.

Throughout the star stayed in the same relative position, appearing to the north-west of them. The Magi were occupied with the daily task of riding safely on the camels, camping, and organising the food. Frequently, they pondered the star's new position in the sky, but they did not have much available time for discussion. Each morning, they were up early to pray. They observed the star daily in the early morning and in the evening, noting its position in the sky.

On the evening of the twentieth day, the star changed its position. The Magi immediately noticed it had moved to their west, so they were not surprised when the legion's commander came to them the next morning to announce that they would now be travelling away from the Euphrates. This would involve travelling in a westerly direction, following some mountain tracks until they reached the River Jordan. Here the scenery became more rugged and there were less trees. However, the commander had obviously followed this route before as he always managed to find a camping place where there was a stream.

The star was not easily visible in broad daylight, but it could be seen very clearly at sunrise, and again after sunset. During daylight it seemed to glow more brightly when a change in direction was needed, but it was still a little difficult to see in bright sunlight so following the star became quite fun. This meant they always knew they were on the right track!

These days were the most difficult, as the track was rough in places, so the commander had to slow down to avoid accidents. They made their way over the lower slopes of the mountains until they reached one of the tributaries of the River Jordan. From there, they began the final phase of their travels, following a star that was now to the south.

This should have been the prettiest part of the journey. The ground was still very rough and dry but there were more little copses of trees and scrubby bushes near to the River Jordan than they had seen since leaving Babylon.

"I think we were right!" Bel-sharra said at this point. "Our main role as Magi is to appoint new kings, and it's obvious now! We're heading straight towards Jerusalem, so we must be going to appoint a successor to Herod!"

"That will go down like a stone boat!" Nabu-naid exclaimed as he reflected on the known plans king Herod had for his successor.

"With Herod, you mean?" Bel-sharra queried.

"Absolutely!" Nabu-naid exclaimed. "In my research I discovered that Herod is very unpopular with the Jews, and he has already prepared for his son to succeed him in power. If we're on our way to appoint his successor, and his successor isn't his son, we could be in great danger!"

"We'll have to make sure our soldiers are well rested before we approach the city, just in case he tries something nasty!" Bel-sharra said thoughtfully.

The Magi called to the commander as they neared Jerusalem. "We've been thinking," Bav-il said. "As we don't know what sort of reception we'll get in Jerusalem, could we possibly travel at night for the last two or three days?"

"Actually," the commander replied, "we can do that quite easily. There will be a full moon in four or five days, so it would be light enough to travel at night."

"It will also be easier to follow the star!" Bav-il observed. The commander agreed. Much as he had been trained for fighting, avoiding it was usually the best option.

Much to their surprise, the star was so bright at night that their little piece of track was illuminated almost as if in daylight. The animals had no trouble avoiding rocks in their path.

They carried on southwards for the next few days, closely following the course of the River Jordan. Eventually, the main track left the Jordan and headed into the hills towards the city of Jerusalem. They followed the path for a day passing Jericho and then going on to a branch in the path just a few miles from Jerusalem, where they took a side path. Now they would be out of the sight of any travellers going to Jerusalem. Here they set up camp and rested for a day. The soldiers relaxed to ensure they were fighting fit for the final entry into Jerusalem, just in case Herod reacted badly and sent out soldiers against them.

"The star has always seem a great distance away," Bel-sharra commented, "but from my daily calculations as we follow it, I would estimate that it can't be more than thirty cubits [14.7m] above the ground!"

"How did you come to that conclusion?" Labashi asked.

"You probably didn't notice," Bel-sharra answered, "but last night I changed my position in our troop several times, and looked at the angle between me and the star. The angle was changing between each of my positions!" The others looked at him, obviously curious about his conclusions. "You see . . ." he continued, after a brief pause for effect, "When I moved further back, the star appeared lower in the sky. But as I came back to the front behind the commander, the star was much higher in the sky."

"Have you been applying the mathematical theories of the Greek philosopher, Pythagoras?" Nabu-naid observed.

"As confirmed by our mathematicians over five hundred years ago." Labashi confirmed, "But yes, I have done exactly that!"

The following day the soldiers got into their battledress, and prepared to go back to the main road that led to Jerusalem.

chapter twelve

A few wealthy travellers would hardly raise any attention as they approached a major trading city like Jerusalem. Travellers and caravans went in and out of the city on a regular basis. Even wealthy-looking travellers like the Magi would not have caused a major stir, except maybe with some traders. There would always be greedy traders eager to deprive the wealthy of their riches through some dubious deal. However, it was a different matter now that a band of very wealthy Magi had arrived, accompanied by a fully-equipped army. In fact, the whole city was troubled by these visitors.

The Magi and their entourage stopped just outside the city and set up a small camp as they considered their next move.

The local people were actually quite excited by the event, although they tried to hide their feelings once they realised their visitors were Magi. Could they really be here to see the unpopular King Herod replaced?

Some dared to approach the heavily-armed group, asking hesitantly, "Why are you here, and what do you want?"

There was a strong element of fear in all those in any way attached to the palace or Herod himself. They knew Herod would not go easily, and if he went then their position in the palace would be in jeopardy!

"Where is He who has been born King of the Jews?" the Magi enquired. "For we have seen His star in the east and have come to worship Him!" Lots of the people were frightened by this, as they could see the possibility of a battle developing just outside Jerusalem.

"We don't know anything about that," the people replied, concluding that this was not what they had expected. A message was sent to Herod who was deeply troubled by the event. He quickly called his chief priests and scribes together and asked them what was happening.

They told him that it was written in ancient manuscripts that one day, there would be a King who would be born in Bethlehem. He would grow up to become the King of Israel.

"This cannot be!" Herod exclaimed. "My son will follow me as the king of the Jews, and his son after him. It's all agreed with Rome!"

"We can only tell you what the manuscripts say," the scribes replied.

"Get out, all of you!" Herod said sharply. "Except you!" pointing at one of the leaders. "I want you to secretly go to the camp they have set up and ask the Magi to come and see me. But don't tell anyone what you're doing."

The scribe surreptitiously visited to the camp and passed on the message to the Magi.

"Can we trust this King Herod?" Bel-sharra asked.

"Can you trust a snake?" Bav-il responded.

"In that case," Bel-sharra said "We must put plans in place so that if anything happens to us, we can be rescued!"

"If we take half of our troops into the city, that should be a big enough threat. He daren't do anything with them in Jerusalem. We could even take a few soldiers with us into the palace to guarantee our safe exit," suggested Bav-il, pragmatically. "And obviously we leave our gifts outside with the soldiers!"

The Magi put on the best robes they had brought with them in case this was where the baby was located. They took a small escort party with them and followed the scribe into the palace. They were led along the plush passages decorated with various weapons until they reached Herod's main hall.

King Herod was seated on a large, very ornate throne. As the Magi entered the chamber, he rose, displaying the toga purpurea he always wore as the emperor. This was a very ornate, woollen garment. It was dyed Tyrian purple with a royal dye which was laboriously obtained from the secretion of many sea snails. Israel was the only known source of those purple murex sea snails at that time, so Rome was very keen to keep possession of the territory, as all the Roman Kings wanted royal purple robes.

"Do you have a new born baby here, Sire?" Bav-il said, showing a little respect for King Herod.

"How did you know about it?" Herod demanded. "I mean the baby of course!"

"We saw a new, special star in the east," Bav-il replied.

"When did it appear?" Herod interrogated, brusque as ever!

"During the Feast of Trumpets, last year," Bav-il replied coolly.

"My scribes claim that the baby you are looking for will be born in Bethlehem. Go there" Herod commanded "and then come and tell me about it so that I can go and worship Him as well."

"We shall to go to Bethlehem tomorrow morning O King."

"I will provide you with an escort," Herod stated firmly.

"That will not be necessary, King Herod," Bav-il stated even more firmly. "We have our own troop of soldiers with us."

"Leave me now! My servants will give you food before you leave the palace." Herod stopped as he reflected on the situation, "Just a minute," he called out. "Now I know you are coming back I will arrange for my cooks to prepare a special meal for you on your return. Now go!" he commanded.

The Magi left and as they went, Labashi looked at Bav-il and asked, "What did you make of that?"

"Not a lot," Bav-il replied. "If it was up to me, I wouldn't go back to tell him anything. But I don't want to start another war! That's why I told him we would be going tomorrow morning."

"But he can watch us go, and follow us!" Labashi exclaimed. "That's true, and that's why we will go tonight!" Bav-il exclaimed firmly.

On returning to the soldiers outside the city, Bav-il suggested that the commander move almost everyone down into the valley, out of sight from Jerusalem. The Magi kept a small band of soldiers with them so that they could appear to set up a camp fairly close to the city. As dusk began to fall, this small group appeared to settle down as if they were preparing to stay for the night. As the sun set, Jerusalem's city gates were closed and the whole town settled down for the night.

The Magi, who had already briefed the soldiers on their plans, quietly packed and joined the rest of the soldiers where they had gathered lower down the hill. Out of sight of the city they were ready for an immediate departure and would leave unnoticed. Two hours after sunset, the Magi gave the word, and everyone quietly slipped away for the two-hour journey to Bethlehem.

"Are we really going back to Herod?" Bel-sharra asked as they set off.

"Probably," Bav-il answered. "But I have been feeling very uneasy about this stage of our adventure, so I'd rather be extra careful."

"That sounds very wise to me," Nabu-naid said, thoughtfully. "An invite to go back for a meal followed immediately by a command to go! Didn't sound very hospitable to me!"

Meanwhile, Herod sent his scribes onto the palace roof with instructions to watch out for any strange, new stars. Unsurprisingly, they did not see a single one! As they were vainly looking sky-ward they totally failed to see the departure of the Magi and their troop. It was not until the next morning that their departure was discovered.

The troop followed the star which led them straight to Bethlehem where they found the city gate opened for them! "How did that happen?" a puzzled Nabu-naid said.

"On this journey, nothing surprises me!" Bav-il said thoughtfully.

"Should we leave everyone out here?" Labashi asked, "and possibly follow the star into the city." They all agreed, so the army and escorts waited outside Bethlehem whilst the four Magi followed the star into the city.

That was when Bel-sharra's observations became even more apparent. The star was so low over the houses that they realised they could tell exactly which turning they had to take, and finally, over which house it eventually stopped.

"Are you sure it's this house?" Nabu-naid asked.

"I think so," Bav-il answered, "but you're welcome to circle around the house and see for yourself."

Nabu-naid did exactly that, returning a few moments later with his observations. "I've never seen anything like it," he observed, "but that star, or whatever it is, really has come to rest over this little house!"

"This little house is not exactly where I would expect to find a special King," Labashi said thoughtfully.

"Not for us to question," Bav-il answered, "so let's knock and find out exactly who is inside".

chapter thirteen

Mary and Joseph had enjoyed their time in Bethlehem. The previous ten months had absolutely flown by. Throughout that time, Joseph had found enough work helping out the carpenter who had been ill. However, now the carpenter had regained his health, and he was ready to take over fully again. Mary had reached the stage where she was prepared to face the people back home, although it was not something she was looking forward to. And Jesus! What about the baby who had been at the centre of the amazing events?

Jesus was no longer a baby, but he was now becoming a toddler. He had grown up very quickly and was walking by the time he was nine months old. He was making very good efforts to communicate with his parents and could usually clearly convey His wishes.

"He does seem advanced for His age," Mary had observed. "Very advanced!" Joseph exclaimed proudly. He may not have been Jesus' biological father, but in his mind he had already fully adopted Him as his own son, and so had a natural pride in His development.

Mary thoughtfully looked at Joseph and then made the statement he had been waiting for. "I think I am more or less ready to face the people back home now."

"That's good," Joseph replied, "because I think my work here will run out in the next week or so." He paused, wondering if he should ask the next question. "Do you think we could start planning to leave?"

"Yes," Mary said thoughtfully. "Jesus is such a little sweetheart, I think He will be the centre of attention when we get back." As she looked at the child she had just put down for a rest, she asked Joseph, "Is your work really running out here?"

"There's enough to keep me going for another week or two. I'm sure I could find more work if I needed to, but I don't want to get too settled. I quite like life in Bethlehem, and although it's great having a big city nearby, I actually miss Nazareth. And anyway," he added after a short pause, "I think I've left dad in charge of the carpentry business long enough now!"

"So do I." Mary reflected quietly. "If I stay here much longer, I will start to think of this place as my home." She looked around at the little room that had become their home. "Now we've made the decision, when do you want to leave?"

"I was talking to one of my customers yesterday," Joseph said, "Do you remember those two large boxes I made for that new family?"

"You mean the storage boxes? The one that doubles-up as a table, and the other as two seats?"

"That's right. Well, you'll never guess! Instead of paying cash for the boxes, the customer was so impressed with my work that he gave me two donkeys. He said that he had stopped travelling and wanted to settle down, so had no need for them. Although they were still valuable, he had two other donkeys for him and his wife."

"So . . . we could actually leave at any time?" Mary said slowly. "And we've got the two donkeys we brought with us." Joseph continued, "So we can load them with all our belongings, and each have a donkey to ride!"

"You're not suggesting that Jesus can have his own donkey too, are you?" Mary chided.

"I hadn't thought of that," Joseph answered smiling. "I suppose we could tie His legs together under the donkey's tummy to stop Him falling off . . ."

"Haha . . .!" Laughing, she paused for a moment, and then continued, "So when do you want to leave?"

"I'm not suggesting we leave tomorrow, or any time as soon as that," Joseph answered. "We've made so many friends here, I'd want to see them all before we left."

"Absolutely," Mary agreed. "There are a few people I'd like to see as well."

"Why don't you give Jesus His last feed so that we can settle down for the night. Life will be easier when He's a bit older and we won't have to stay up for His evening feed."

"Yes, his evening feed is definitely getting earlier and earlier each day" Mary said encouragingly.

Before anything else was said, there was a knock at the door. "Who can that be at this time of night?" Joseph stood up quickly, and opened the door. "Oh, my goodness!" he exclaimed.

"Who is it?" Mary asked without turning around.

"You'd better come in!" Joseph said as he backed away from the door, bowing deeply as he reversed into Mary.

Mary gasped, "Who are you, my lords!" she exclaimed.

Bav-il and Labashi had just entered the room, and she could just see Nabu-naid and Bel-sharra through the open door. Each Magi was dressed in his best and most-decorated me'il. A white linen sadhin [under-shirt] showed through the open front of each me'il. Over their shoulders, they each had a highly ornate adderet mantle. Joseph and Mary were both speechless! Joseph had only ever seen one person wearing an adderet on a visit to Jerusalem, but Mary had never seen one before.

"We are Magi, Magistratas from the Upper House of Megistanes in Babylon," Bav-il said very regally.

"Most of our group are on the outskirts of Bethlehem, but we have come in to see your baby," Labashi said reverently.

Mary turned and lifted the sleepy child from His bed, and held Him out towards Labashi. "How . . . How did you know about Him?" she asked hesitantly.

"We saw His star in the east," Bav-il answered, "and through prayer and research, we discovered a very special baby had been born. Now we are here to worship Him."

Mary really wanted to bow down in front of these awesome visitors. She tried a little bow but it was difficult with the child in her arms. However, before she could balance Jesus suitably, these powerful visitors were kneeling down in front of her.

"You said that you followed a star to find Him. How is that possible?"

"That we cannot tell you," Bel-sharra answered. "All we can say is that we saw a star last year, about the time of the Feast of Trumpets. It seemed to have very peculiar characteristics, and it actually led us specifically to this house. I know that sounds impossible, but all I can do is tell you what happened." He paused for a moment, then looking straight at Mary he added, "So perhaps you can tell us something about this baby, and why He is so special?"

Between them, Mary and Joseph explained everything that had happened to them since the visit of the angel Gabriel, around the time of the winter solstice almost two years previously. As they finished their tale, Bav-il sent Nabu-naid to bring in the gifts.

"We didn't want to bring these gifts in until we were certain that this was who we had come to worship. You have to admit this doesn't seem to be the likeliest place to find an important baby King!" Bav-il said as he handed the gifts to Joseph. Joseph thanked the Magi profusely as he accepted them, in awe of what was happening.

"One of the most important jobs we have in Babylon is to appoint kings," Bav-il continued, "and it is something over which we have absolute authority." He paused as he looked again at the child, "This child is going to be one of the most important Kings ever on earth and we have brought you gold to honour His Kingship."

"We have also brought you frankincense, which is a very unusual gift to give to a king. We believe He will not only be a king, but He will also be a high priest," Bel-sharra said reverently.

"In the whole of recorded history, there has only ever been one person who has been awarded that double honour. And that person is Melchizedek who was a king and a high priest. Your child is also going to be both king and high priest" Labashi said as he gently stroked the little boy's cheek.

"We have been highly honoured by YHWH to be invited to see Jesus," Nabu-naid said solemnly as he handed over the third gift. "This is myrrh. We don't know the significance of this particular gift as it is a spice associated mainly with death. But it was what God asked us to bring, and so we have brought it."

The Magi spent some time squeezed into the tiny house, praying and worshipping the little boy. Then they departed, returning to their troops for the night, and leaving Jesus' family to settle down at the end of the day.

The Magi had no sooner settled at the troops' camp, when all of them were suddenly woken. "I've just had a terrible warning," Labashi said, wide-eyed. "We must leave, and we must leave now!"

Nabu-naid woke up with at the same time and exclaimed, "I've just had a terrible warning!"

"I just said that!" Labashi loudly asserted. Bel-sharra and Bav-il both sat up too, instantly wide awake. Both confirmed that they also had just experienced very worrying dreams.

"We must wake everyone up, and leave immediately!" Bav-il exclaimed. "That little child is in terrible danger, and we mustn't tell Herod where He is. We must get everything together as quickly as we can. We need to be completely out of sight from Jerusalem in the morning."

"And," Labashi cut in, "we must also go back home by a different route! That's what I was told."

The Magi quickly packed up and the leader of the troop got everyone organised and mounted for departure. Soldiers are very good at responding quickly to a change in circumstances so they were soon on their way. The moon was almost full, illuminating their journey so that they made very good progress. Halfway through the next day's journey, they found a suitable crossing over the River Jordan. Going back to Babylon this way would be slower, but their route would be much more difficult to follow. They didn't stop until the following evening and despite their slower speed because of the rugged, mountainous track, they were well away from Herod and his soldiers by nightfall.

Back in Bethlehem, as soon as the Magi had gone, Mary and Joseph settled down for the night. However, they had no sooner fallen asleep when Joseph was wide awake!

"Mary, Mary!" he exclaimed as he shook his wife awake. "I've just had a warning from an angel. We must leave at once! Jesus' life is in great danger!"

"What do you mean?" Mary asked as she struggled to wake up.

"An angel appeared to me in a dream," Joseph said urgently, "and he ordered me to get up. Then he told me that I was to wake you and Jesus immediately and take you both to Egypt. It sounded very urgent. He said we had to escape!"

"Escape? What from?" Mary asked sleepily.

"Herod! The angel said that Herod was going to search for the child so that he could kill Him! So you need to get up quickly, and get Jesus ready." Joseph whispered sharply.

Kill her child? Kill Jesus? The very thought had Mary dressed to travel, packed and ready to leave in minutes. "It was lucky you got the donkeys organised the other day," she said.

"It wasn't luck!" Joseph retorted, "No, it's God's hand on our little boy. He knew that this was going to happen. He allowed everything to fall into place so that Jesus would be safe." He looked around their little home for the last time.

"Have you got the presents the Magi brought?" Mary asked. "Of course!" Joseph replied, "Those will be essential on the journey, and very useful after we arrive in Egypt."

"How long will we have to stay there?"

"I don't know, but the angel told me he would come and tell us when it would be safe to return."

Joseph helped Mary onto one of the donkeys, and then handed Jesus to her. "If I lead at first" he said, "your donkey will follow mine. You won't have to worry about where we are going. Once we are a good distance away, and its light, I can carry Jesus."

"Agreed," Mary replied, and the little family set off. Joseph wanted to look back at Bethlehem, but he was too focused on the task in hand to look. For the first night, the moon was almost full and they made steady progress. Like the Magi, Joseph had decided that apart from 'comfort' stops, he wanted to travel for the whole of the next day before stopping at an inn.

"Stopping at an inn?" Mary had questioned. "They're quite expensive, you know."

"Not a problem," Joseph replied. "The gift of gold was actually gold coins!"

"So we can stay at an inn every night, can we?" Mary asked enthusiastically. A few nights in comfort! That was something to look forward to.

"We should be travelling for about twenty days," Joseph answered, "so I'm sure we can stay in an inn every night whenever there is one on our route. Jesus must have the best we can give Him!"

"And then what's going to happen?" Mary enquired.

"We'll have to wait and see," Joseph responded. "But we have quite a few gold coins. In fact, we have more gold coins than I have ever seen, so we could live on them for a year or so!"

With that, their journey to Egypt continued.

chapter fourteen

Herod straightened the folds on his toga. "The Magi should be back later today," he said, with a sneer. "Worship another king? They'd have to be fools if they thought I'd worship another king!"

He got up from his throne, and started pacing impatiently around his room. "I wonder how long they'll stay in Bethlehem?" he said to himself. "I can't see them wanting to stay too long." He paced around the room again. "After all there's nothing in that little town to keep them!" Then he shouted, "Julius!"

"You called, sire," Julius entered the room. He was Herod's personal guard and was always dressed ready for battle. He was wearing a silver cassis [helmet], and body armour of overlapping iron strips covering his red woollen under-shirt. He was based in the palace so wore sandals rather than the heavy-soled military caligae [shoes] worn for battle. The only battle he expected here was with his boss, the king!

"Have the Magi returned yet?" Herod asked impatiently.

"No, sire. Are we expecting them to be here for the evening meal?"

"Yes!" Herod snapped, "I invited them, so they should be here! They wouldn't dare refuse my invitation!"

"Should I send out a welcoming party to meet them?" Julius requested cautiously. The last thing he wanted to do was upset Herod when he was in a bad mood!

"No! Just tell the guards on the wall to let me know as soon as they are in sight. Now go!" Julius left, and communicated Herod's instructions to the guards before resuming his duty outside the throne room.

Herod repeatedly summoned Julius almost half-hourly until dusk. Eventually, as the city gates were being closed, he was called for the final time that day.

As Julius entered the chamber, Herod was angrily pacing backwards and forwards. "Where are those Magi, Julius?" as if Julius should know! "At dawn, I want you to send a handful of lightly-armed soldiers to Bethlehem to . . . er . . . remind the Magi that they're expected here for their evening meal with me tomorrow."

"Yes, sire." Julius replied, then withdrew. Thankfully he was not called again that night.

The next morning, he arranged for a few fast, lightly-armed soldiers to remind the Magi of Herod's invitation. The soldiers returned on very tired horses in less than three hours.

Julius took their report to Herod. "Come!" Herod called in response to Julius knocking on his door. "Well, were the soldiers successful in delivering my message?"

"No, sire!"

"No? No? What do you mean by no?" Herod barked back.

"The soldiers reported that the people in Bethlehem did not see the Magi either arrive or leave. A very few saw a troop of soldiers stop outside the walls after the gates had been shut for the night, but that was all. By the morning there was no sign of the visitors, so they presumed they had just stopped to rest for the night."

Herod was really angry to hear this news. "Send a legion along by the river, and tell them to make great haste. They're only a day behind, so they should be able to catch up with them. And summon my scribes to me." He commanded.

Sensing Herod's dark mood his advisers entered very circumspectly. "You heard the Magi, didn't you?" Herod demanded.

"Yes, sire," they answered.

"You heard when they first saw the star, didn't you?" Herod continued.

"Yes, sire." The chief adviser answered.

"Well," Herod challenged, "when was it?"

"A-a-about t-ten m-months ag-go," one finally stammered.

"Right!" Herod paced around his chamber, then suddenly stopped. "Send for my garrison commander!" he ordered.

On hearing the mood Herod was in, the commander rushed to Herod's chamber as quickly as he could. "Yes, sire!" he said as strode into the chamber.

"I want you to send about twenty lightly-armed soldiers after the Magi." Herod commanded, "They will need to be mounted for speed. The Magi have not returned to me here as I ordered. Do everything you can to bring them back. If they refuse to come, then find out from them where they went to worship the baby king. Don't be too aggressive as I told them I wanted to worship this new king. If you seem aggressive, then they may realise what my real intentions are . . ." He paused for a moment as he considered his next move. "Then I want you personally to take a troop of soldiers to Bethlehem because I want the baby King found and killed. He will be about ten months old."

"How will I know who it is?" the commander enquired.

"Well . . ." Herod thought for a moment, "The Magi were convinced that he'd been born about ten months ago . . ." He paused, "but it is possible he'd only just been born, so he could be any age under ten months . . ." He paused again whilst he collected his thoughts. "But how will you know and recognise a ten-month-old baby boy? I know! We'll put in place a safety net! I want you to take soldiers to Bethlehem immediately, and kill every baby boy in Bethlehem under the age of two. And include all the surrounding districts. That way, I will know that I have got Him!"

"Once people hear what we're doing, all the babies will suddenly be two years old. How will I know their age?" the commander questioned.

"That's easy! If you or your soldiers can understand a lot of what the child says, then they are over two. If you can't understand them, then they are under two. Now go! Go!"

"A voice is heard in Ramah,
Weeping and great mourning.
Rachel weeping for her children
And refusing to be comforted,
Because they are no more"

Jeremiah 31:15 & Matthew 2:18

chapter fifteen

Once they reached Egypt, Mary and Joseph found a very pleasant inn and decided to rest there for a few days. "Are we going all the way to Cairo?" Mary asked after a few days.

Joseph thought carefully for a few moments, but before he could reply, Mary asked again. "Did you hear me, Joe? Is Cairo going to be our next home?"

"I'm sorry, love . . ." he paused. "Yes, I did hear you, but I just got a sudden funny feeling!"

"Nothing to do with me, I hope," Mary joked.

Joseph smiled and gave Mary a little hug. "It's like I don't think we need to go any further, but I don't know why."

"I suppose we could stay at this inn for some time," Mary said quietly.

"We could stay for a year or two with all our gold coins!" Joseph replied, "But I don't think we're going to need to stay that long. Anyway, we know what we have to do, don't we, my love?"

"Yes. Jesus is God's Son, so we just have to trust God to provide for us all until we get home again."

Only a short time later, Joseph had a very powerful dream in which an angel visited him. The angel told him it was now safe to return to Israel. The next morning, Joseph passed on the good news to Mary.

"But are you sure?" she responded.

"I am certain," Joseph answered. "The angel spoke about the people who massacred so many babies to make sure that Jesus would also be killed. The angel assured me that the people responsible are now dead."

"That sounds like a fitting end for them!" Mary exclaimed. "But if we return, we must be careful, just in case you've got it wrong." Joseph raised no objection to the caution Mary had suggested.

The couple started making all the arrangements to start their return the next day. Later that evening a caravan stopped at their inn for the night and Joseph discovered that it was heading for Jerusalem.

"That's quite a coincidence, isn't it?" Joseph said, tongue-in-cheek.

"Do you think God might have had a hand in the timing, Joseph?" Mary answered playfully.

"That is a distinct possibility," Joseph teased, "so we'd better be ready first thing in the morning. I'll go and find the leader and ask if we can join his caravan."

Not surprisingly, they were welcomed to join the caravan, and set out for their return to Israel the next morning.

Herod the Great had been ill for some time, but he did not live very long after ordering the death of Jesus. He died from a chronic kidney disease that suddenly worsened. Following his death, his region of rule was divided into four areas. Three of his sons each inherited control of one area, and his daughter Salome inherited control of the fourth.

As they were approaching Jerusalem, another angel appeared to Joseph. The angel warned him not to go to Jerusalem because Herod's son, Archelaus, had succeeded Herod in the south. Obeying, Joseph led Mary away from the caravan and they continued in a north westerly direction, heading towards the sea, and the little sleepy fishing village of Ahuzat Bayit (now Tel Aviv). They could then go from fishing village to village until they reached the valley north of Caesarea that would lead them back to Nazareth. In this way, the prophecy was fulfilled about Jesus, that 'He would be called a Nazarene.'

Mary, Joseph and the little Jesus returned to Nazareth. Mary became a house wife, and had several more children. Jesus grew up with His brothers and sisters, and Joseph worked as a carpenter. The next record we have of Jesus is of Him going to Jerusalem at the age of twelve. Little else is known until He started His ministry at the age of thirty.

To find out other things recorded about His amazing and miracle filled life you will have to read the books of Matthew, Mark, Luke and John in the New Testament section of the Bible.

AD 1996

In 1996, three Christian ministers went from England to New Zealand on a ministry tour. They all felt that one particular church was the most important of all the churches they were booked to visit. At the start of the journey to this church, a thick fog suddenly fell. At that time, they were driving along winding roads through the mountains. They realised immediately that they had to go so slowly that they couldn't possibly get there before the meeting started, and actually, they'd be doing well to even arrive before the meeting ended. They thought of giving up and turning back, when one of them posed a searching question.

"Do we really believe God wants us to get to that church meeting?" he challenged.

"Yes!" they all agreed.

"So it's up to God to get us there! Let's pray and ask for God's help!"

So that's what they did!

Within a few minutes, the driver thought he saw a motorbike headlight approaching the car from behind.

The light reached the back of the car, passed through the back window, and hovered in the car for a moment. All of them felt overwhelmed by a total calm and peace in the car. The light then passed through the front windscreen, and hovered in front of the bonnet. The driver realised that the light was somehow inviting him to follow. He started tracking it, driving at a speed that would have been suicidal under any other circumstances. As they dropped over the brow of the last hill, the mist cleared and the light disappeared. They arrived at the church just as the meeting was about to start.

The minister giving this testimony said that even with the benefits of his education, there was only one word that would describe the light they followed, and that was 'Star'! It was like following a star!

If Jesus could send a 'star' to help three ministers find a church, how easy would it have been for God to send a star to lead the Magi to Jesus!

The minister giving this testimony said that after the event, they phoned each other every few days to confirm that it really had happened. My wife and I heard this story spoken at a large Spring Harvest meeting in Minehead.

footnotes

Where was Mary?

According to Luke, Mary stayed with Elizabeth for 3 months – to the time of the birth of John. In some translations, it is inferred that Mary may have left just before the birth. This would have excluded the birth of John from the narrative. However, as Elizabeth was in her 6th month when the angel visited Mary, and it would have taken Mary about a week to get to Judah. If she stayed with Elizabeth for 3 months she would have been there for the birth. I have chosen to have Mary leave just after the birth so that the details of John could be included as part of the story. As a caring relative, I could not imagine Mary leaving before the birth.

Birth dates

In Israel and in many other countries, dates of birth have never been considered to be as important as they are in the West. Consequently, birth records tend to be inaccurate. The calendar was also changed to zero at the birth date of Jesus, but early calculations were not very accurate. Most records give the year of the birth of Jesus as about 4 BC, based on the historical records of Josephus, a historian some years after the life of Jesus. His calculations were based on an eclipse occurring in March, 4 BC, shortly before Herod died. However, this eclipse seems to have been on Dec 29th 1 BC.

When consulting other records, Jesus seems to have been born in the 41st year of the reign of Augustus. Herod's death has been more accurately calculated to have been January 14th 1 BC. There are also records of Jesus having been born 28 years after the death of Cleopatra, and, according to Eusebius, in the 42nd year of Augustus. These events all point to a birth in the autumn of 2 BC. However, the important thing is that He was born, He lived as a man, and He died to pay the price for our sins. That really is the only important thing.

Purple dye

The cloth-makers used a purple die obtained from sea snails that only existed on the sea front at Caesarea in parts of Israel. These snails apparently could not be found in the area after the sacking of the temple by the Romans in AD 70. In 1850, a young chemist tried to synthesise quinine, but instead, produced a sticky, black mess. He tried to dissolve this in alcohol, and accidentally produced a very good purple dye. As a result, the snails were almost forgotten until recently when a lady in Tel Aviv was cleaning her fish tank. She left the water on a window ledge in the sunlight. A day later, she had a jar of purple dye!

Ha-Kotel

The records of the Ha-Kotel [the Western, or Wailing Wall] indicate that the wall was built around 20 BC to 18 BC, although it is not clear when it was fully completed. Records indicate that it was originally built to a lower height than it is today. Also, it was not completed until after the death of King Herod. The tunnels have been known about for some time, and can be visited. However, the synagogue is a very recent discovery.

Although Jerusalem has been destroyed and re-built nine times, Ha-Kotel is a highly-revered site. It is the only original part of Jerusalem that survived all the sieges and destruction that Jerusalem suffered.

Temple steps

Some of the stone steps have also survived. In this story, Mary sat on those stone steps leading up to the temple (Chapter 3). From there, Mary would have been able to look over the large olive grove in the valley below. That olive grove is much smaller today, but a few of the olive trees in it are believed to be over 2,000 years old. So those trees would have actually been growing as young trees at the time of Jesus.

www.3dworldministries.com